MOBILE MAYHEM

Mary Lu Scholl

ISBN -13:9781704505992

DEDICATION

This is dedicated to my loyal dog who died very shortly after the cover picture for the previous book was taken, but before it went to print. I miss him very much, every day.

I have met a great number of wonderful people in the creation of this series. None of the characters I have created represent anyone. They and the situations are all products of only my imagination.

TABLE OF CONTENTS

CHAPTER 1

HARD CHOICES

Henry regretfully handed over the jewelry he had carefully rolled up into the plush towel to the lady with the carefully permed, gray hair and the glasses that hung around her neck on an ostentatious looking chain. Everything else about her was subdued, serious, understated. That chain was different.

She saw him staring at it and explained. "I have an eight-year-old granddaughter. She made it for me for Christmas. I'm not sure how much longer I'll wear it, but I will for a while."

"I'll get the most out of these pieces that I can." She continued smoothly. "I certainly understand how much you need it. I haven't seen Jessica for quite a while, but you did say she has gotten considerably worse." She glanced through the one-way window she used to keep an eye on the store when in her workshop. Jessica sat quietly flipping through a magazine that was upside down. "Medical care is so expensive anymore."

She lifted a pearl choker with gold appointments. "This is lovely. Not quite antique, but old enough that I'll call it heirloom." There was a squash-blossom in quite a different style, silver and turquoise from the southwest. "You don't see a lot of southwestern jewelry out here; this will be distinctive."

The woman continued her commentary as she picked up and catalogued the pieces, making out a receipt for him at the same time.

She focused on him once more. "If you give me thirty to sixty days, I can do better than in the ten days we discussed."

The indecision on his lined face was clear.

"Just let me know in the next few days if I can take longer." She sighed and followed him back to the lobby, where she tried to speak to Jessica.

Jessica looked right through her and tried to put on a watch she picked up from the counter. Henry gently removed it and handed it back to the sympathetic woman. He tucked the receipt into his wife's voluminous purse.

He nodded and mumbled "Thank you." His hands felt light, his heart heavy, as he walked out the door.

CHAPTER 2

ROSE MARIE

Whatever it was rocketed out of the shrubbery and the next thing I knew, my cocker spaniel, Buddy, was climbing the oak tree. Maybe not exactly climbing it, but making a good stab at it.

A woman clambered through the same shrubbery and tried to follow both the dog and the cat, who was now straddle-legged a few feet over the dog's head. Not an accomplished climber, the cat's paws had gotten progressively farther apart and now it couldn't move any farther up and was afraid to come down.

I grabbed Buddy's collar and pulled his front paws back down to the ground. The woman reached up and pulled the kitten loose. A shower of bark hit Buddy's head (adding insult to defeat) as the bark came loose instead of the kitten's claws. Hedge-crasher cuddled the frightened cat and looked over at me.

"Oh! Potato Woman!" I heard her exclaim under her breath.

"Potato Woman?" I repeated, because I really didn't understand the reference.

She blushed and it matched the pretty pastel abstract print of her house dress. A horrified expression took its place. She had a very pretty perm in her blondish-gray hair. She was not quite my height – she was maybe five foot four. I outweighed her by about fifty pounds.

Maybe more.

Pretty blue eyes sparkled, where my brown ones were somewhat shifty (according to my second husband). Right now, mine were probably flashing at her evasive look. I was getting an inkling I had a nickname I didn't know about.

"Potato Woman?" I repeated again and waited.

She was valiantly trying to come up with a reason that didn't involve my stature, my weight or my wardrobe. "I'm sorry; I thought you were someone else."

I laughed. I had to give her points for trying. "Right." Since the appellation was probably apt, I let her off the hook. "Let's start over, then. I'm Patty Decker." Sometimes known as Double Decker, but I wasn't going to volunteer the information and get THAT nickname started around here. Potato Woman was bad enough.

"I'm Rose Marie. It's nice to meet you." She soothed the kitten by holding her securely and rocking gently, crooning when she wasn't talking to me.

"Is the kitten yours?" I called it a kitten mostly because of its obvious inexperience in climbing. It was a rangy little gray thing; but most of the feral cats around here were about the same size. This shaggy little thing was being comforted by her, not struggling, so she was familiar to it.

"Oh no. She's not mine. I just happened by and saw her run up the tree."

My eyes narrowed and she blushed again. "Just being a good Samaritan on a walk through the poison oak and creepers in the woods beside the park?" I scoffed.

She deflated just a little. "I put food out back here and stick around a little while to make sure they get a chance to eat it without predators coming around."

"Wouldn't it be easier to feed them on your carport, for instance?"

"I used to. The park rules say I can only have two cats. They define "have" as "feed." She put the kitten down.

Buddy was no longer excited by the cat and just reached over with his nose to sniff at it, earning a quick hiss and a scratch. He backed up and sat down, looked up at me. I could read his thoughts as clearly as I could have heard them from a person. “Mom! What did she do that for?” I comforted him with a quick pat.

“So, I gather you have two and there are more?” I continued the conversation. “Stupid rule.” I added just so she would know which side of the argument I fell on. “I love cats.” I only had one right then; I’d had to put Patches to sleep a few months ago.

“They aren’t really mine. I gather up new ones when they turn up, and have had all of them spayed or neutered. The vet around the corner gives me a pretty substantial discount. I have to feed them away from the park, though, or I'll get evicted. Not very many people have caught me back there; but it's not in the park, anyway."

She brushed off her dress, hiking it up a little to turn a pocket inside out where some twigs and leaves had fallen when she crashed through the undergrowth.

"Wait a minute. Isn't there a cat lady closer to the front of the park, Cassandra, Catherine..."

"Carlotta. She's been here for a hundred years and her cats are grandfathered in." She looked at me again. "You usually walk down the old road. What are you doing over here? Not that you can't walk anywhere you want." She added hastily.

Grimacing at the reminder of why I was changing our habits, I explained. "Two houses down from the park a Neanderthal has started letting his dogs out loose in his front yard. He doesn't have a fence and Buddy, here, doesn't have any sense of self-preservation. So, we've had to change stomping grounds."

"Where do you live? Inside the park, I mean." I asked her. "I live in a travel trailer in that little alley cul-de-sac with a couple of other small RVs."

"I live in the third mobile from the end on the full-time side of the park."

I knew already that the park divided itself into three groups, within two sections.

Just like in school, there were some who rigidly tried to enforce the distinctions.

There were the full-time people, separated only by attitude and custom from the snowbirds who were interspersed but only here in the winter. Both those groups were mostly domiciled in mobile homes of various sizes, shapes and state-of-repair. They were also, mostly, on the west side of the amenities. Amenities consisted of the laundry room, the clubhouse, the gym, the pool and the shower rooms. Horseshoe pits and shuffleboard areas were set between the paths from one side to the other.

On my side, the east side, there were a few full-time residents, like me, but mostly RVs, and a lot of people who were snowbirds but came and went with their RVs.

I tried to picture which mobile home was hers. There was one that was separated from its neighbor by a big, old oak tree with a swing. I had noticed it specifically because there was frequently a little girl swinging on the swing. I had never stopped, just nodded, because I lived on the other side and wasn't comfortable enough yet to try to breach barriers, however artificial. "You live next to the little girl who swings all the time."

"There's a swing, yes, that blows in the wind a lot, but I've never seen a little girl there."

She looked a little puzzled.

"Maybe I have the wrong house." I didn't think so, there weren't very many children here. It was supposed to be an "Over 55" park with a few exceptions in the RV side, but being over 55 didn't mean you weren't raising children anymore. Not important right now, though.

"Now that I know where you are maybe I'll see you around." I smiled and turned to go when I remembered. I turned back.

"Really? Potato Woman?"

She was already disappearing back through the hedge and pretended she hadn't heard me.

Obviously, the name hadn't originated with her. Or had it? It had to be a commentary on my shape (squat, like a serving of mashed potatoes) or my sense of style (bland and shapeless, like a serving of mashed potatoes). I certainly didn't have thin skin. Nor was I half-baked or par-boiled.

Still; it was irritating. I was on a diet; that would show them.

I continued through hostile territory. I hadn't really thought much about it before, but now sadness washed over me as I felt judged and unwelcome on this side of the park.

Maybe I should just walk out of the park and on the other side, down Highway 44 to the east.

Damn. I had just started to feel like I belonged and was beginning to like Florida. Now I was sad again.

I had moved here almost a year ago and set up camp on my son's property. Just as I got comfortable, he got a transfer.

"Nothing personal, Mom." He assured me as he moved back up north. To be entirely fair, he did suggest that I go with him. Let's see... cold weather and a son who is always at work and likely to move again... or warm weather among people my age who weren't going anywhere (until they died). I picked warmth.

Not long after I moved here my neighbor was killed. Since I am an aspiring writer, I stuck my nose into it and wound up solving the case.

Some of the killer's friends still snub me. Like the maintenance guy, Pete. Others were just shocked. Most of the others (on my side of the park) seemed to accept me at face value.

So, I wondered, who named me Potato Woman?

As I passed the Jaxsons' trailer I spied Jessica. She was a distinctive little woman with bright red hair and shaped like a Sandhill Crane, skinny and angular. I had only encountered her once or twice. She never attended any of the park functions, and rarely even left her porch or yard. She had a somewhat vacant expression as she looked off down the road toward the west.

I stopped, and without preamble asked her. "Hey, do you know who named me Potato Woman?" She turned abruptly and her finely featured face was suffused with confusion. She turned to escape into her tropically feathered nest, without a word. Despite the walls of the porch being only screen, the vegetation planted in pots inside and all around the outside gave the suggestion of expected privacy. She and her husband had a pair of enormous talking birds in their private jungle.

Maybe I should have led up to it, instead of just blurting it out. I actually wanted to know her better. Okay, I wanted to know her birds better; they were fascinating. I gave Buddy a light tug to take his attention from the parrot that was whistling and chucking at him. As usual, it occurred to me too late that I could have been more polite or circumspect and gotten a better answer.

I was trying to become more socially acceptable to the polite southern society, but it was a slow process.

CHAPTER 3

ALBERT

I was relaxing after my oatmeal breakfast. I read that oatmeal was a good diet breakfast. It was probably better for me without the raisins, the brown sugar and the cream. It wouldn't have tasted as good, though, so I probably wouldn't have eaten it. Then what good would it have done me? Better my way.

Albert was sitting in one of the fold-up chairs across from me, seated on my glider. He was often about when I was on my little patio. Surrounded by a six-foot wooden fence on two sides, my twenty-five-foot travel trailer on the third side, it was open to where I parked, partially blocking the west side. It was filled with plants and covered by a six by eight vendor tent. It was just secluded enough for an anti-social writer.

Albert had kind eyes and patrician features. He would have been a very attractive man if he had been alive.

Albert had a trailer parked year-round next to me. He had been a snowbird who actually arrived about the time I moved in. We had gotten off to a rocky start.

Okay; I was obnoxious. There was a conflict that I had survived and he had not.

No. I didn't kill him. A lesser man may have blamed the messenger, as they say, when I discovered who had killed him. Now, we were friends and I wished I had known him better before he died.

Unfortunately for him, I was the only one in the park who could see or hear him. He was not my first ghost, so maybe it was a matter of practice or exposure. Both my last two husbands had died on me. They both hung around after they died. Don, however, I didn't see as much after I married George. George, I hadn't seen since I moved from Colorado back to Florida.

I had been overheard talking to Albert upon occasion, and was getting a reputation for being a little touched – even among the neighbors who seemed to like me – so I had to be careful who might hear us when we were outside.

I started to ask Albert about the girl in the swing on the full-time side of the park but stopped just in time to peek first through the boards to see if anyone was close enough to hear me. All was clear.

“What do you know about a little girl who swings on the big oak tree toward the south end of the dark side?”

“I’m sure you misspoke and meant to say the west side, right?” He answered reproachfully. He was gently trying to improve my manners. “I haven’t been over there much since, you know.”

It was still a sore subject, his poisonous demise.

“I don’t remember seeing a little girl at that end. I can certainly look.” He answered but continued to sit back with his arms crossed behind his head.

“Well?” I prompted. Why hadn’t he gone to check? We had been chatting already for several minutes and had run out of anything new to say.

He opened one eye. “Impatient, are we? Just because I go to check – at your behest, mind you, doesn’t mean I have to come back and tell you anything. Honey, dear girl, honey gets better results.”

Chagrined at being caught out again as rude, I picked up my knitting and prepared to wait – patiently.

He winked out and came back. "She's a little girl who lived here when the first house on this acreage existed. She died when she was eight but has no idea what of. Eight-year-olds are pretty clueless about the world around them. The mobile home park has pretty literally grown up around her. She seems to be attached to that tree and the immediately adjacent mobile homes, or maybe she's just most comfortable there. You are probably the only other person in the park who can see her."

"Her name is Dahlia." Albert added. "And, since you are clearly bored with my company..." He disappeared.

Great; now he was going to pout. Who knew when I'd see him again?

"Good morning." Nathan came around the corner with his big black dog. "What's new in your world?" He asked genially.

"Do you know Rose Marie, over on the other side?" To my amazement, Nathan blushed. What was it lately? Everyone seemed to be embarrassed about everything.

"Yes. I think I've met her a time or two. Why?" He asked warily.

"I just met her yesterday. She seemed a little paranoid. She feeds cats way out in the woods because she's afraid she'll be evicted."

"She's not paranoid." He said defensively. "They are always trying to get rid of her over something stupid!"

"Who are? Why? She seems like a very nice woman to me."

"I don't know her that well; I just hear stuff." He mumbled.

"Have you heard me called Potato Woman?" I demanded.

"Can't say that I have. Why would you think so?" In spite of asking a question he started drawing farther away. "Gotta go. See you later."

That was distinctly odd. Normally he could talk the socks off of ...I couldn't think of anyone in Florida who wore socks. A sock-monkey. That was as good an answer as I was going to come up with.

Buddy brought it to my attention that it was time for a walk. I reached in the door to the trailer to drop my bowl in the sink and grab his leash from its hook. I almost fell over the baby gate I keep inside the screen door. It was to discourage the cat from getting out into the wild, cruel world. She had no front claws and grew up in an urban environment; she had no clue about predators, so she was much safer inside.

As soon as we hit the rip-rap drive I touched my gums with my tongue and headed back to the trailer for my teeth. I needed at least the upper ones or my face looked funny.

Damn, that means I didn't have them in when Nathan was here. Albert didn't count. I never knew when he was going to pop in, so I had given up on dignity or decorum where he was concerned.

I did, however, ban Albert from the trailer until I was up and dressed in the morning. He had startled years off my life the first time he showed up at my breakfast table, at six in the morning, without warning. Oh, and he was not allowed inside after dark in the evening unless the door was open or by pre-arrangement!

I turned on my current audio-book to listen to while we walked, and we set off. This time we stayed on my own side of the park and took the road that takes off behind the businesses on the highway. It's rural and quiet. There were turtles and bugs.

On our way back we drew close to another walker with a little mop-dog. I was sure it was a pedigreed something or another, but it was still a little black mop-dog. Its bark sounded like a squirrel. Still, I pasted on my friendly face and shortened Buddy's leash.

"Good afternoon." She offered.

I nodded politely. "Is your dog friendly?"

"He's an angel." She let out his leash and I let Buddy get a little closer.

Quick as a wink the little mutt snapped at my dog. I reacted by yanking him back and knelt down to put my arm around him and put me between them in case she hadn't pulled hers back fast enough.

"Oh. I am so sorry! He's never done that before!" She pulled the offending animal with her as she backed down the road in the direction she had come from.

Buddy stayed behind me the rest of the way home.

Albert popped in as we made it to the quasi-privacy of my patio. "Don't you believe it. That little long-haired rat has bitten every friendly hand in the park."

"I blame the owner." I unhooked Buddy and let him jump up the stairs into the trailer.

"I heard you ask Nathan about Rose Marie." Albert offered.

"Do you know her? Or, rather, did you know her? Which is correct, anyway?"

He shrugged. "You're the English expert, why don't you write a lexicon as it applies to the paranormal? Then we'll both know!" He grinned. "I did know her. Not well. Perhaps knew of her is more correct."

"More correct?"

"If you want me to talk to you, quit interrupting."

There was a ruckus in the tree over his head. A bird apparently took flight abruptly and the squirrel farther out on the branch got bounced and fell to the ground. Squirrel, acorns and leaves fell to the ground right through Albert. I couldn't help it. It was funny.

I laughed. He left.

My computer was mocking me. I had finally written a somewhat factual account of Albert's demise and the excitement of solving it.

I had taken literary license with the main character (me) as in I modeled myself after Jessica Rabbit. No one was going to call her Potato Woman.

The story came out pretty well and was now sitting on the digital shelves of Amazon and Kindle.

So. Now what?

I needed a new story. I had started listening to a show on a podcast (is that how you put it?) about weird things that happen in Florida. Surely, I could come up with some inspiration from that. It was really pretty boring around here lately.

Buddy and I checked the mail to see if there was a letter from my son, then took off for town. My son preferred to write letters, he said he couldn't talk to me on the phone because I'm hard of hearing.

I don't know what he's talking about.

CHAPTER 4

MARTHA

The next morning was quieter than normal. It took me a few minutes to figure out why. The Jaxsons' birds normally contribute to the cacophony of birds and squirrels by mocking them. Every squeak, call, trill or squawk got repeated by her beautifully feathered mimics. As Buddy and I walked past on our one hundred and three steps to the dumpster it was quiet and dark on their porch. The urban assault vehicle that Henry Jaxson normally drove was gone.

It occurred to me that if I had seen Jessica, I could have apologized for being so abrupt yesterday. More likely, though, if I had seen her, it probably wouldn't have occurred to me.

Buddy pulled me towards the grassy area dividing the dumpster from the clubhouse and pool. I allowed him to choose our return course, it was his walk, after all.

As we neared the west road (I really needed to learn the proper names of these streets) I started to look for the trailer I thought was Rose Marie's. We turned the bend at the far south end and I could see the little girl swinging, even as early in the day as it was.

The people on the dark side stay up late socializing and can't get up at a reasonable hour in the morning.

That was entirely tongue-in-cheek. It was really mind-boggling to listen to the chatter at Bingo, for example. It was "they this" and "they that". All manner of unpleasant or unacceptable attributes were applied (equally) by each group of residents to the other.

But I digress, the point was, there was no one around, and I could stop and whisper to the little girl.

"Dahlia? I'm Patty. This is Buddy and it's nice to meet you." Buddy tried to barge through the profusion of flowers to sniff at our new friend, but I held him firmly. Whoever took care of these flowers wouldn't appreciate his big feet trampling through them.

The little girl started and formed an "Oh" with her lips. She disappeared and left the swing swaying gently behind the blooms.

"I guess we startled her, big guy. If no one else around here talks to her, we must have scared her. We'll have to take it slowly."

The next mobile home, if I was right, was Rose Marie's. A cat dish sat by the back door inside the screen room – so it was some cat lover, anyway. It was well kept and neat. The flowers in the front yard must have been hers. No one else in the park had such a display of blooms and fronds.

There were flowering pots everywhere and lush natural growth between them. It was glorious and I had to stand still and admire them. Buddy focused on a honey bee and I gently nudged him away from it.

"You must be new, here." The voice was right behind me.

I turned and was face to face with a large, not fat, just large, woman pulling a bicycle trailer with a small cat and an even smaller dog zipped inside.

Buddy thought that was cool! Canned company! His stubby little tail wagged so hard his rear end danced as he sniffed them through the net.

The woman who had approached was taller than I and was wearing the ubiquitous outfit that you find on Blair.com. It was all pastel and matched perfectly. The pants were solid and matched the flowers all over the crew neck t-shirt, one of the flowers was prominently displayed on the breast of the matching sweater. Even the bicycle trailer matched.

Which came first? The trailer or the shirt?

Why is my first response to some people catty? Maybe I really am the bitch my second husband called me when I divorced him. I prefer to think I have instant discernment. I do have manners, though, when I remember them, and she might actually be a perfectly pleasant person in every way.

Like Mary Poppins, I pasted on a smile. "Kind of new. I live on the other side in a travel trailer. I'm not a snowbird, however, I have been here since last summer. I'm Patty."

I gestured in sweeping admiration to the garden next to me. "I was just admiring these flowers and wondering how she managed to get them all to bloom so early. I haven't been here long enough to have a handle on what normally blooms when, but these are beautiful."

"Have I seen you at Bingo? You do look a little familiar." She sniffed. "Well, if you're new you don't know. She may be good at plants by she's no better than she ought to be. You don't want to know her if you want to get along here."

She was obviously waiting for me to ask her why. No better than she ought to be? What kind of epitaph is that?

"Who else should I avoid?" I asked her accommodatingly.

She eyed me sharply – not a stupid woman, then. She was trying to decide if I was mocking her or agreeing to take her unsolicited advice at face value. "You'll get to know. Why don't you sit with us at Bingo this week and we can get to know you? I'm Martha."

Apparently, she decided I wasn't smart enough to ask her "why." She was willing to see if I would be an asset to her group, there being no question that they were good enough for me.

"I'll see you there, I've only been a couple of times, but I want to go more often." I assured her with my fingers crossed. "Thank you!"

She headed back toward the highway and Buddy and I, having had enough of the dark side for the morning, turned back toward our own home.

It was much later when I was listening to Rat Pack Radio and washing up after feeding myself and my animals that I remembered I had questions Albert might deign to answer.

I'm not sure why I felt comfortable asking Albert practically anything. Maybe because there was no pressure of a relationship. Maybe it was just because he was so non-judgmental. Was he always that way? Had he mellowed after he died? Would he even know?

My outer door was latched open, baby gate inside the screen door. I called him to see if he was around and would answer. "Hey, Albert?"

He popped in and was sitting behind me at my little dinette.

"Hey! What's up?"

"What do you do when you're not talking to me or doing things like checking on Dahlia?" I asked him, suddenly curious.

He didn't answer right away and I stopped and turned to look at him and see why.

He was sitting comfortably (how can a ghost get comfortable?) and looked surprised that I'd stopped and turned around for an answer.

"What's the matter? Is it some ghost-secret of some kind; I'm not allowed to know?" I sounded disgruntled and knew it.

He grinned at my impatience. "No. Usually when you ask me something like that it's in a fit of impatience and you don't really want to hear the answer. You just interrupt and go on to whatever you want from me. I was just saving my breath."

"You don't have breath."

"So to speak." He was still grinning at me.

Okay, he was right. It's hard to hear your rudeness pointed out to you, even with a smile.

"I'm sorry." I was a little defensive, though. "So, what do you do?"

"It's hard to describe. So now I have to admit that even if you didn't skip past my answers, I would have to change the subject to avoid answering."

We both laughed.

"What's up, Pats?"

"Two things, actually. Why is Rose Marie a verboten subject? She seems like a very nice woman, I like her. Nathan turned the color of a red-headed woodpecker when I mentioned her. The other is – do you know who nick-named me Potato Woman?"

"Rose Marie is a very nice woman. If I hadn't had Muriel around, I probably would have availed myself of her company."

"Availed yourself? She sounds like a prostitute." I interpreted his response with a small frown, not of censure, just curiosity.

"Not at all!" Now he frowned at my interpretation. "You may have noticed that she is attractive: face, form, and manner. She is the perfect mature wife. She cooks wonderfully, bakes superbly. She sews, mends and knits. She is willing to watch fishing, racing, boxing, football or horror movies while she does so. She is good company."

"She is discreet, and cuts hair." He added after a slight pause. "She has a lot of friends in the park." He struggled to explain further. "Most of her friends are male."

I laughed. “No wonder the women don’t like her.”

“You might be less than circumspect, but you are perspicacious.” With a saucy wink he popped back to wherever it is that he goes.

“Hey! Where did Potato Woman come from?” I raised my voice, not at all sure that raising my voice made any difference in his time and space, but I was frustrated and getting nowhere with that line of enquiry.

CHAPTER 5

TENANT ASSOCIATION

There was a meeting the next day at the clubhouse. I had avoided these meetings since I moved in. Actually, I hadn't even known about them for quite a while. When I did, it was only because it was on the calendar posted on the bulletin boards of all the buildings a few days ago.

This calendar is pretty and professionally done and only updated October through April. The rest of the year the residents were expected to know what was going on.

Tenant Association Meeting 10 am

I asked Nathan about it when he came by with Angie later that morning. "What is a tenant association? I know about Homeowner Associations, but never one of these."

"It's where the full-timers get together to resolve issues in the park."

"Does the owner or the manager come to them?"

"No."

"Then what possible good is it?"

"Well, I never actually went to one. My wife, Betty, used to go to them. She said they all got together with their complaints and took what they called resolutions to the manager."

"There's a meeting Tuesday at 10 am." I sipped my coffee. "Do you want to go with?" I laughed at his startled look. "Would you like some more coffee? I'm just curious, is all," I assured him, "not looking for trouble."

Nathan turned down the coffee and left shortly thereafter. Mention of Betty invariably left him depressed even this many years later. I was sorry she had come up. Nathan was a very nice man.

Albert showed up in his wake. "Some people just quit living when they lose a spouse."

"Did you?" I asked. Albert rarely talked about his own past.

"Divorced. She left me. I let her file for divorce, it was the gentlemanly thing to do. Even so, I rarely saw my daughter after that. Once her mother had divorced the next husband, my daughter contacted me, but a twenty-year gap is pretty difficult to get past. Too much water under the bridge."

"She is apparently still paying the rent on your trailer. Do you have any idea what she plans to do with it?"

"I paid the rent a year at a time. She has a while to decide." Now he looked sad, too. I should just learn to keep my mouth shut.

"Are you really going to that meeting?" He asked me.

"Thought I would. I'm curious after Rose Marie mentioned the rule about cats. I know there were a couple of pages of rules when I moved in but I don't remember paying any attention to them and certainly didn't keep what I considered extraneous information."

"Have fun!"

Poor Buddy felt betrayed when I left him home alone. It was 97 steps to the clubhouse, not all that far, I assured him.

I was one of the first to arrive. There were only three other women when I got there early, on purpose. The idea was to get a good seat. That meant level, padded, and not in front of the bathroom.

I spoke to the other women but only received civil nods back. I sat down and they stopped talking even to each other. Finally, I went into the bathroom to see if my hair was combed (as good as it gets) to see if my shirt was on inside out (tell me you haven't done that) and to see if I had my teeth in.

I was pretty sure I heard a reference to "Potato Woman" when I came back out, but that might have been paranoia on my part.

I decided not to push the issue. There was a new arrival who also looked around uncertainly. When the others ignored her, I got aggravated.

I walked up and introduced myself as "Patty" and asked her name. Albert would die if he saw me giving lessons in manners.

Well, he would if he could.

"Cheyanne. It has two 'e's and an 'a'."

"That sounds like you say it a lot." I smiled.

"Well, my parents couldn't spell; what do you do?" She shrugged. "I just moved in a few days ago. I'm renting a mobile home towards the front of the park."

"I've been here several months, but this is the first time I've come to one of these meetings." I settled and gestured to a chair next to me. People had trickled in and there were fifteen women and one man.

I was not surprised to see that the meeting began when Martha arrived and that she was the one behind the table. Looking officious, she actually used a gavel to call us to order.

"This meeting is called to order. Doris, can you tell us what we discussed at the last meeting?"

Doris, a heavy woman with support bandages wound up both of her calves to the knees started a laborious effort to stand.

"No need to stand up, we know how difficult it is for you." Martha interjected. It might have sounded solicitous from someone else. From Martha it sounded like a catty commentary on her size and condition.

"We talked about the noise from the wind-chimes. We talked about the cigarette butts in the common areas. The hedges behind space 105 needed trimming. We also discussed whether planting lots of flowers to encourage butterflies could be considered a breeding program, quite properly prohibited by our rental agreements. Also, the mobile home in space 42 is deplorable and needs to be dealt with."

I almost choked over the butterfly thing. There were lots of yards with plants, and some had flowers, but they had to be referring to Rose Marie's yard. Were they jealous?

Martha stood up to address the list. "I took our concerns to the manager. The hedge behind space 105 has been trimmed."

There was polite applause.

"The cigarette butt issue is one we need to address with each other and with offenders as we see them. The park has supplied plastic fire-retardant receptacles conveniently in each common area and by the doors. I am assured they are emptied regularly."

"I move we establish a committee to make a schedule to watch for offenders and institute a fine." A querulous voice from the rear suggested.

"The manager has nixed the fine proposal in the past. I don't think we need a committee, just bring the names of offenders to my attention."

I heard names bandied about and wondered who was going to have their windows soaped or their yards toilet-papered that night because they smoked.

Actually, I hated the cigarette butts as well, but after the butterfly thing I was not prepared to support any of their initiatives.

“There is bad news about the wind chimes. Unless we can prove they violate the decibel level prohibited, they stay.”

“I also regret to say that when I brought up the butterfly propagation issue, the manager had the temerity to laugh at us.”

Apparently eager to get past the two failures, she forged on without waiting for a response. “Space 42 is available for rent.

Its condition should improve with habitation."

Cheyanne raised her hand a little meekly.

"Yes?" Martha called on her with the imperiousness of a Catholic School nun.

"I've just moved into space 42. What exactly do I need to do to meet your expectations?"

"You've just made a step in the right direction." Martha's expression was then one of beaming benevolence. "If you will see me right after the meeting, I will make a list. Now. New business?"

"I think too many bees is a safety hazard."

"Noted. Doris write that down."

"That Jaxson woman is still sitting in front of her house during the day and writing down the names of everyone who walks by. Isn't it a violation of some law to make a record of someone's activities without their permission?"

I looked, but couldn't see where that one came from.

"I will call the Sheriff's Office and ask for certain. I do want to point out, however, that we all know Jessica is rapidly losing ground mentally. I would bet that if you actually looked at her tablet you wouldn't be able to read it anyway. Also, her husband is never very far away; she's harmless."

Another voice commented quietly. "If you had a ne'er-do-well for a husband you would likely cultivate a few weird habits, as well. The only thing Henry ever did right was to marry her. Spends every last dime they have on brainless investments. Very sad."

"Those birds! He was going to breed them. Bought two males."

The lone man in the room stood up.

"Yes, Ralph?" Martha recognized him. "Change of subject?" She sounded hopeful.

"It's getting to be spring again. Last year there was a problem with huge floaties in the pool. No one could actually swim because of all the little inflatable islands – couches, beds, tables, etcetera that covered the water. Can we see about a "no floatie" time or a percentage of water reserved for swimmers, maybe with a roped off lane?"

Several women were apparently of floatie citizenship and spoke in outrage on behalf of their territories.

Martha raised a hand to calm them all down. "All in favor of a "no floatie" time, keeping in mind it could conceivably be at any time during the day, please raise your hands."

There must have been more than a couple of quiet swimmers, or at least fair-minded people, in the crowd. With a burst of fairness, Martha declared it a resolution. "I will take it to the manager and see what needs to be done."

Cheyanne rose when I did to leave, and trailed me out the door.

"Aren't you supposed to be seeing what Martha wants you to do to your house?" I asked, my emphasis leaving no doubt as to my opinion of being told what to do by this bunch.

"Tomorrow will be soon enough." She rolled her eyes.

We were just reaching the driveway when a woman with penciled in eyebrows and dyed brown hair, in an unfortunate cut, shouldered past us. She turned abruptly and some of her double-knit outfit turned with her, some did not, and was twisted around her waist. Judy? Trudy? That was it, Trudy.

"I know you're only paying half as much rent as the rest of us because you solved that murder." She sniffed knowingly and dared me to refute it.

How do things like that get started?

"I don't pay rent at all, but I try not to spread that around to you unfortunates who have nothing to bargain with." I smiled at her. I didn't really care what they thought they knew. It was fun to go along with it and see her expression.

Cheyanne looked at me curiously as the woman huffed off.

"Complete garbage. I pay as much as anyone else for my space rent. It was fun to see her expression, though. Didn't you think so?" I giggled; I couldn't help it.

"Murder?"

I sighed. "Last fall one of the men in the park was poisoned, Albert Cross.

Anyway, I helped the Sheriff's Office solve it." Enough of that subject. She got points for focusing on that rather than the rent, however.

"Let me know what they want you to do at your space. Do you live alone?"

When she nodded assent, I offered help. "I might be able to help, or at least find you help."

"Should I paint it Kelly green and purple?" She looked mischievous.

I liked her already. "Are you going to Bingo tonight?"

She considered. "I think I've had enough of that crowd this week. Maybe next week if you're offering an invitation to go with a friendly face?"

"Okay. The maintenance guy, Pete, does side jobs. He does a good job but doesn't like me. Offer him pastry. Don't mention Potato Woman."

"Potato Woman?"

"Apparently my nickname." I gave a little wave.

CHAPTER 6

CHEYANNE

It turned out the swimmer was Ralph. "No floatie" time was now between five and seven a.m., every day. It was duly posted at each door at the pool, the shower house and the clubhouse.

It seemed that Ralph was Martha's sister's brother-in-law. That was apparently close enough to get his request approved, but not close enough to get actual daylight hours.

He worked part-time with a turf management company and was best friends with Henry Jaxson. He was often on their porch helping Henry dream up another get-rich-quick scheme. All this was according to Nathan. He wanted to know about the meeting even though he hadn't wanted to go.

How did Nathan know everything when he never seemed to socialize with anyone but me?

Later, Albert laughed at the bird story. "I hadn't heard that one. I heard he invested in Edsels."

I looked askance and tried to remember my history as I scratched Buddy's left ear. "What year was that?" I asked suspiciously.

"Okay, okay. Maybe not Edsel, but I did hear, though, that he invested most of their savings with that Bernie Madoff Ponzi scheme. And, unless he's fed them all to his wife to try and stop the Alzheimer's, he has a whole closet full of "Natural" (Albert made air quotes here) vitamins that he tried to sell in a pyramid scheme several years ago."

Cheyanne poked her head around the corner of my fence.

Albert had long since quit disappearing every time I had company. He was now comfortable being invisible. It did make it a trifle difficult to talk, sometimes, trying to keep one eye on his expression and body language while listening to whoever stopped by.

"You must be Albert?" Cheyanne asked.

If blood could drain from a bloodless face, it did.

"I am. You are...?"

"I'm new here. Patty told me about you yesterday. Not that you were a ghost, but that you were murdered."

She put a hand over her mouth. "I'm sorry. Was that rude? I know you haven't been gone all that long, it must be a painful subject. Most ghosts I meet have been older...gone longer...from another time..." She floundered.

Albert gathered his wits about him. "No offense taken. I was just a little surprised that you can see me. Other than other ghosts, and Patty and Buddy, here, no one else seems to see me."

"I think everyone can, they just don't. I had my grandpa close at hand when I was growing up and am comfortable with ghosts. He stuck around until I turned 21 and then he went into the light or whatever you guys do when you finally leave us behind for good. There have been a few others for me. The last house I lived in had a very unhappy woman ghost." She rolled her eyes. "I didn't live there long."

"I seem to be unrestricted here in the park. That's my travel trailer over there. I stay pretty close to it, or am over here, most of the time."

"He's very welcome here." I added somewhat extraneously to the conversation. "Would you like some Kool-Aid?" I asked Cheyanne.

"Sure. I just came over to report on my meeting with Miss Martha about my new home."

A pickle jar of Kool-Aid in the cup holder on her chair, she settled in to visit with us.

"I knocked on her door this morning. She was a little frosty because I ditched her after the meeting last night. You need to explain Rose Marie to me, by the way."

She waved her hand as if to say – later. "Martha kept me waiting on her steps while she got her shoes, a sweater and – honest-to-goodness – a clipboard."

Albert laughed; I grimaced.

"She actually led the way back to my house. She stood in my driveway and told me the siding probably needed to be replaced, but that as a renter it was unlikely I would do that, so a good cleaning would have to do. Paint the trim. Pull the weeds. Redo the stepping stones to the front door, they're a safety hazard. Then she started on my blinds and drapes." Cheyanne had been counting prospective chores on her fingers.

She stopped to take a sip of Kool-Aid. "Root beer? That's different!"

Cheyanne continued. "Then she marched up the steps to the side door and waited like she expected me to let her in to dissect the interior next!"

"I told her I would see about the blinds and drapes. But I had the décor inside to take into consideration, and that was more important to me." She gestured in a kind of toast. "I had to stand right in front of her in the doorway and thank her for her time and expertise or I would have found myself replacing moldings in the closets! The inside was just too much not her business." Outrage was clear in her voice as she ran down.

"Whoever owns the trailer really should pay to get the exterior cleaned or painted – it really does need it," Albert opined.

"Rose Marie can point out what plants are weeds and which ones are flowers. She's a very nice woman who is not exactly on the popular list around here. You heard about her at the meeting – the bee propagator. She fills an interesting economic niche as housework fill-in person for some of the men in the park. They are generous to her, and the single women in the park are jealous of her success. They seem to regard her as competition, but she doesn't want a man to keep!"

Cheyanne wrinkled her brow as she made the same assumption I had. "You mean she..."

Albert interrupted with a wry look. "Trust a writer to put in extra material and leave out the important stuff. No, she's not, she just does housewifely type things and they help her ends meet."

"Why Albert! That's the first time you ever called me a writer! What brought that on?"

"Self-published or not, available in print makes you a writer," he admitted; then promptly disappeared to avoid continuing the conversation.

"Cheating!" I called quietly and Cheyanne laughed.

"How about the stone path; what do you think?" She continued.

"Well, she called it a safety hazard and I honestly wouldn't be surprised if someone would trip on purpose, to make a point, if you get on their bad side. You did make points by inviting the queen bat to give you her opinions, however."

"Do bats have queens?"

"I'm not really up on flying mammal monarchy. However," I continued, "if there is no path it can't be a safety hazard. You don't have to have a path; just pull up the stones and toss them into a corner.

"Devious! I like it!" Cheyanne finished her drink and stood up to go.

"About Albert..." I started.

"Understood. I've been ostracized before for the same thing. I will only speak to him when we're alone."

"If you decide to ask Rose Marie for help, she's the one with all the flowers (easy to find). Tell her Potato Woman sent you." I grinned.

She laughed back as she patted Buddy on the top of his head. “The bug breeder.” She chuckled.

CHAPTER 7

MARY JANE

Cheyanne did indeed ask Rose Marie to help and she said she would, but it would have to be Sunday.

She did try to warn Cheyanne. "You must realize that if I help you do anything, whatever it is, it will undoubtedly be wrong."

"Don't care."

We stood back and admired her yard when we were done. Cheyanne had decided not to cheat with the path. We had pulled up the flagstones, dug down, levelled and replaced them carefully, filling in around them with sand.

An unexpected rain shower practically cemented them in.

There were quite a few native flowers. "It looks great! Thanks guys."

All three of us stood with hands on hips and admired our work.

We made a motley crew.

Rose Marie had gone to the grocery store early because she had baking to do later. Sunday was a day she tried to keep to herself and she loved to bake. Her self-imposed image meant she was wearing a floral house dress. She did have cotton gloves, and her hair was pinned up carelessly.

Cheyanne wore jeans and a slinky T-shirt that said “Soft Shoulders” on the front and “Slippery When Wet” on the back.

I wore my ubiquitous nurse smock (pretty, cotton, cool, washes well, has large pockets) and shorts (thorns ruin pants, I’ll heal).

I laughed at us.

Space 42 gleamed in the sunshine and put her neighbors to shame. Of course, that in itself was another transgression, but what the heck.

“Kool-Aid break at my house.” I wiped my hands off on the back of my shorts and turned to lead the way.

"I can't." Rose demurred. "I really have to get started so my breads can rise properly. Then I have my own laundry and mending that I have put off. I'll take a rain check, though."

"Okay. You're excused this time, but we want apple fritters tomorrow morning!" I warned her and looked at Cheyanne.

"I'm coming. Just let me change my shirt and I'll be there in a minute." She waved at Rose Marie. "Thank you, Rose!"

We were sipping in the shadow of my spider plants when Albert joined us.

The peace was shattered by the Jaxsons' big birds. Cheyanne jumped, startled.

"It was quiet without those birds for a few days. They must have boarded them somewhere while they were gone." I commented. I glanced over to Albert. "You ought to tell Cheyanne about them."

Albert launched into the story of the unfriendly birds who cussed at him when he sat on his own porch, across the driveway from them.

"Do you have any idea where they went?" I asked him about the Jaxson's latest trip.

"Do you really think they would confide in me even if they could see me?"

"Well, I guess not. But you are in a unique position to eavesdrop on anyone you want to," I pointed out.

Albert looked pained. "I know you didn't like me when I was alive, but I thought you had formed a better opinion of me since then?"

"Sorry." I told him, and I was. Then I explained to Cheyanne. "I didn't really know him. I had heard bad things from a neighbor who didn't like him, and then I heard the birds cussing at him, and allowed their opinions to sway mine. He was, or is, a very nice man."

Apparently, I was forgiven when Albert just continued. "I wouldn't be surprised if he took her to see family, or a doctor. She had gotten noticeably worse very recently." The very nice man who didn't eavesdrop pointed out.

"She is probably suffering from Alzheimer's Syndrome." I explained the general consensus of her friends and neighbors who knew her better than I did. I had just overheard them.

"I heard her family wouldn't have anything to do with them after she married Henry. His children gave up on him a long time ago, and hers consider him a fortune hunter who has decimated her assets," Albert volunteered. "Just gossip among the guys. You have to admit, though, they never have company. Also, they never go anywhere; which makes this trip very odd."

"I've heard that some people are claiming that marijuana slows the Alzheimer's process down." I put in, having seen it on the internet recently.

"I don't believe it. I have a girlfriend in Colorado whose daughter sells it. It's legal for even recreational use, there; they can grow it, too." Cheyanne put in.

"I thought Cheyanne was in Wyoming," piped up Albert.

"Ha, ha. Anyway, the owners of the company have claimed it cures everything from the common cold to cancer. Seriously, Arthritis, you name it. I honestly think they are just trying to expand the market to be so big that it will have to be legal everywhere, sooner."

"Legal to take or not, it's still unlawful to grow here. Even if you get a use card, your medical insurance won't cover it. So, you have to pay for it yourself, and it is so outrageously expensive here that it is out of reach to most people." Albert quoted a price and Cheyanne let out a low whistle.

"The park manager, Jeremiah, is supposed to take it for his eyes but can't afford it. He's a great guy, but he can pinch a nickel so hard the buffalo poops."

Cheyanne and I both cracked up. "I never heard that one before!" I managed to get out between gasps.

"So, does he get it from the underground or black market or whatever they call it?"

"Don't look at me," Albert answered her. "It's not part of my world. I just remembered the conversation a while back."

Albert popped out with a little wave as Nathan came around the corner and I introduced him (and Angie) to Cheyanne.

A thought suddenly occurred to me. "Hey, Nathan. Do you know where the Jaxsons went?"

"I'm pretty sure they went to one of the Mayo clinics. Pete said a cousin of his sold some jewelry for Henry and he said it was for medical bills and he was going both to the Mayo clinic and to a holistic treatment center in north Ocala that Jeremiah recommended." Nathan looked thoughtful. "He did say they wouldn't be gone long because he had work to do. Don't know what, though. Nobody I know would hire him, even if he could leave Jessica alone long enough."

It was always interesting to hear the provenance of Nathan's gossip. I was beginning to appreciate two things. Never,

ever tell anyone around here anything you didn't want known. Also, be careful who you talk about, because if the other person isn't related to the subject by blood, they are related to them by marriage.

CHAPTER 8

BIRTHDAYS

“You have no idea how much time is spent on buying, stocking, preparing, eating and cleaning up after food, until you don’t have to do it anymore,” Albert commented. “Still, I miss sitting down to a good meal, or even just a peanut butter sandwich once in a while.”

"What was your favorite meal when... you know?" I asked.

"I liked sushi. I loved steak and potatoes." He winked out.

Have I mentioned how effectively it changed the subject when he did that?

Buddy and I needed to get something for the birthday celebration at the clubhouse that afternoon. I no longer had time to cook.

When we drove by, Jessica was standing out in front of her SUV, glaring toward the west.

"Good morning, Jessica." I made a special note to be polite to her after all I had heard about her history with the errant Henry.

It made no difference. She ignored me completely and went back inside.

"See, Buddy. I'm not the rudest one in the park."

Rose Marie flat refused to go to the birthday party (held once a month for every one having a birthday that month), but Cheyanne said she would go with me.

I wanted something different to take for a snack. Almost everything I had seen brought to the clubhouse was baked and sugared, or fried, or both.

I settled on sushi. My favorite was Spicy Tuna. I wanted three kinds, so I also took the Dragon Roll (eel and avocado) and the California Rolls for the less sophisticated palates. Buddy didn't even sniff it on the way home. Absolutely no interest in raw fish. Go figure – he rolls in fertilizer given half a chance.

"What's the difference? I asked. He just thumped his tail because I was obviously talking to him.

Carrying the selection arranged on a pretty plate I walked the 97 steps to the clubhouse. Buddy was home comforting the cat, Ashes, for missing out on the fish.

There were at least thirty or forty people there. There were oohs and aahs over the food. The tenant association provided a cake each month; a half of a sheet cake in the summer, a full one in the winter.

I noticed people looking at the sushi but not trying it. I told Sally, the Bingo checker what was in them and she spread the word. Finally, a few began to try them (mostly the men) but I still heard some affected sniffs from some of the women.

Cheyanne and I sat off to one side. A few women stopped to comment on the weather or how improved space 42 was, but no one sat down. Cheyanne brought merengue cookies, some lemon, and some chocolate.

Martha finally stood up and tapped her glass with a spoon.

How she rated a metal spoon when the rest of us had plastic, was beyond me. She probably carried it around in her purse with her gavel.

"Has anyone seen Jessica or Henry? It's Jessica's birthday this month and I thought I saw their car back. They may have forgotten, with the trip and all."

"I actually saw Jessica, but not Henry." I offered.

Ralph also spoke up, "I saw Henry headed somewhere early this morning, but I was going out to breakfast and he was too far away to speak to."

Martha picked someone seemingly at random. "Doris, pop over there and see if they forgot, please."

Doris started to reach for the walker she had used to get there. Cheyanne reached over and patted her hand. "I'll go."

She sent a glare at Martha and I actually saw several people look at Cheyanne approvingly.

"She's the bird lady, right?" She whispered to me.

"Yes. Do you want me to go with you?"

"Nah. You stay here and keep the natives from getting restless." She patted my shoulder.

As soon as she was out the door, I heard a voice bring up the new flag on the wall. "Where did the Marine flag come from?"

"It was donated by Fred. He's a retired Marine." An anonymous voice replied.

"Why don't we have a Navy or an Army flag?"

"Because no one has donated one."

"Well, someone should."

Opinions bounced around like a Jack Russel Terrier. They traveled much too fast for me to even try to identify the speakers.

"I don't think we should have a POW/MIA flag. It's depressing and this is a place of entertainment."

Dead silence followed that statement. One man left.

Conversation ensued after a minute or two, but at lower decibels and in smaller groups.

Cheyanne came back and stopped to talk to Martha, then continued back to me.

"Jessica was on the porch but wouldn't answer the door or speak to me. When I persisted, she threw a glass at the door. I waited to see if Henry would come out but he didn't. I suggested to Martha that she should call and see if he answers the phone."

I looked over her shoulder and Martha was pressing numbers on her phone.

She listened for a minute without saying anything and then motioned for Ralph to get up. Like any good squire, or knight in shining armor, for that matter, he headed out the door.

It was time to go, anyway. Only about half the sushi was gone, so I decided to see if Rose Marie would like some left-overs.

Cheyanne and I wandered over with them and a few cookies. My hands were full, so Cheyanne, after she looked curiously about the door frame, knocked for us.

"I can't get used to the no doorbell thing. That and the fact that absolutely no one uses a front door. Some of these homes don't even have one!" She just shook her head.

Rose Marie answered with a smile and flour up to her elbows, so we just left the goodies and went our separate ways.

CHAPTER 9

RALPH

As I drew closer to home, I saw commotion at the Jaxsons' house. Ralph had either been let in by Jessica or ignored her protests and went in anyway. She was screaming "Get out! Get out!" The birds were equally upset and squawked loudly and cussed at the top of their little feathered voices.

While I watched, he went into the main house with Jessica trailing after him hurling invectives.

I waited to see if he was going to get out unscathed. Besides, I was curious.

So, sue me.

After a few minutes he came out the door again and put the birds in their cages with treats, and pulled the cage covers over them. Then he gathered up some scattered toys and rehung a rolling pin on two chains that made it into a big-bird size swing. He muttered under his breath and fetched a pitcher of water to fill both water bowls and then spilled some seed into their trays.

The birds finally shut up. Jessica seemed to have run out of steam; or maybe she just changed her mind. Who would know? Now she seemed to be willing to cooperate.

He asked her where her old cell phone was. "I know you don't have a landline, and Henry isn't here with his phone. You used to have a cell phone; do you know where it is? Or, do you know where you keep a list of important phone numbers?"

Jessica started muttering about burglars, Nazis and government spies, then she stomped off into the house. She clutched her voluminous purse close to her chest to keep nefarious hordes away from her. Ralph followed and came back out holding a small notebook. He left the porch and came outside.

"Henry is nowhere." He explained to me. "He's a lazy SOB, but he never leaves Jessica alone anymore. If he wanted to run an errand without her, he would call Lucy."

"Lucy?" He spoke into his phone. "Have you heard from Henry? Jessica is alone."

I could hear a voice raised on the other end of the invisible line.

"Thank you. I'll call her daughter."

He looked at the notebook again and called another number. "Justine Smithers? You don't know me but this is Ralph and I live at the park where your mother and dad live..."

"Sorry; your mother and her husband." He continued. "Your mother is alone and we can't find Henry. I think something is wrong."

And impatient voice carried but I couldn't make out the words as clearly as I did her tone.

"I can't leave her alone, and we don't know that he will be back. Something is wrong," he repeated.

"I'm not sure how long it's been since you talked to your mother, but leaving her alone is not an option. I'm going to have to call the Sheriff's Department to come get her if you can't come. She won't go with me. Lucy, the girl who usually..."

Interrupted again, he explained. "Lucy lives here in the park, but is out of town and can't come look after her."

Another pause.

"I can't put her on the phone, she's locked herself in the bathroom."

Another pause and I could hear an angry tone.

"I'm sorry. I can stay here until you come if you are coming now."

"No. Two days is out of the question. I'll call the Sheriff's Office and see that she is taken somewhere safe. I'll take care of the birds, however." He hung up and I could see he wanted to throw his phone at someone, probably Henry.

He started to search for the Sheriff's number.

I rattled it off for him. Sad state of affairs when you know the Sheriff's number by heart.

He thanked me and called it.

I listened as he told the story to the dispatch officer; he was nodding at her responses even though she obviously couldn't see him do so.

Albert appeared at my shoulder, but I couldn't talk right then, he would have to figure it out on his own or wait. After Ralph hung up I walked home to get Buddy and his leash to come back. Albert followed me and I filled him in as I unlocked the trailer and let him past the puppy-gate inside the screen door.

"I haven't noticed Henry, either." Albert said and we headed back.

Ralph was still looking anxiously into the trailer but was off his phone and pacing.

"Do you want us to walk to the front of the park and give them directions? You know that GPS is all but worthless in here."

Fortunately, he assumed I meant me and Buddy, since I'd slipped and included Albert in my offer.

"That would be great. I don't want to leave in case she does come out." He resumed pacing.

We met the Deputy out front and gave him directions.

After that we were pretty much superfluous, so we went back to my space to sit on the porch.

CHAPTER 10

DEPUTY CHARLIE

"Honestly, if Rose Marie is such a good cook, how can she recommend this vile concoction for breakfast?" I complained as I gagged, but still drank most of the green drink. I poured the rest into Buddy's dish and laughed when he turned up his nose. Smart dog.

"Kale, it's not for breakfast anymore." I cheerfully mis-quoted as I went back in the trailer to rinse out my glass.

I had gotten the ice from the big icemaker at the clubhouse. Being cold was supposed to improve the taste. Not.

There was a knock on the skin of the trailer and I started to yell at whoever it was to come back at a decent hour. Then I realized it was after ten in the morning.

I had been writing my newest novel – for the umpteenth time - and had been on a roll when I stopped for my smoothie.

I sighed and opened the door the rest of the way for Deputy Charlie Johnson. He was a baby-faced officer who had once knocked on my door in the middle of the night to ask me to turn my television down… But that was a different story.

I noticed that his mustache had filled in a little more.

"Well! What can I do for you? You'll notice I'm not playing the television, but I have been listening to Rat Pack Radio..."

"Can you come out and talk with me, please? Or should I come in?"

"I'll come out." Have I mentioned that I live in a shoebox? Anyplace I want to step, I have to step over something; Buddy, a cat, a water bowl...

"Can I get you something to drink?"

"I'm good, thank you."

I sat on a folding chair and left the glider to the uniformed kid with the long legs, who probably would not be able to get out of the folding chair.

"It's about Mr. and Mrs. Jaxson. No one has seen Mr. Jaxson since early Sunday morning. Have you seen him, or have you spoken to Mrs. Jaxson and she mentioned him?"

I laughed... "I'm sorry. I know it's not funny, but if you have spoken to Jessica Jaxson you would know that is pretty pointless. No; I haven't seen him and she did not speak to me about him." That was all I really had to profess.

"Ralph Emerson said you were there when he called the daughter, and then us."

"I was. I couldn't hear her side of the conversation, of course. I gathered, though, that she was less then helpful. Poor Ralph was just trying to get help for Jessica."

About that time there was a coughing fit from the Jaxson's porch. Deputy Johnson looked over, startled.

"Just a bird." I dismissed the noise. "Have you talked to Lucy? She babysat the birds while they were gone. Her roommate had a terrible cold and the birds have been mimicking him ever since."

He looked at me seriously. "How do you know it's not sick?"

"Don't ask me. That's between Ralph and Lucy. I was concerned and asked him, but he had already called Lucy about it.

"Do you know anyone else we should talk to?"

"Now how would I know that unless you tell me who you have talked to?"

I took pity on him. "I would talk to Jeremiah, the park manager. Pete is the maintenance guy, try him. Also, Martha is a busy-body and knows everything – just ask her."

He looked like he was trying not to laugh. He must have already met her.

"Really, they kept to themselves." I continued. "Good luck. If he's been gone this long, either something dreadful happened to him or he's a scoundrel that none of us really knew."

Albert took the Deputy's seat as soon as the young man stood up to leave. As he backed the hundred or so feet down the rip-rap drive I felt free to talk.

"You know; he's not even a missing person, yet. On top of that, he's an adult and can legally walk away from his life."

Albert pointed out that he could be brought up on charges of neglecting an elder person at risk.

"Good point, but she's safe right now. It is really hard to believe he would walk away after carrying on for so long. He really has cared for her for quite a while. Which," I pointed out, "is a credit to his character, but also a reason to reach his limit and disappear."

"I still think someone should be looking for him," said Albert firmly.

"Could he have just left?" I decided to take the possibility seriously. "That girl Lucy left rather conveniently. Do you suppose he went with her? Both looking after Jessica, her young and vulnerable, him stressed and feeling old and restless, it could happen. Or, if he had any money, he could have just walked away, I suppose."

"Lucy seems like a steady sort. She lives in the temporary area because she is too young to live back here, but it is a big trailer and she has a roommate." Albert contributed.

"Is she back, yet?"

"I don't know." He winked out and came back a few minutes later. I was petting Buddy's soft ears and trimmed fur – my cloud dog - and talking to him about the vagaries of human nature.

"She's back, but only just." He informed me. "Her car is in the parking spot with the trunk open and she's carrying bags inside."

"Maybe I should to visit her. I could ask her something about the birds for an excuse. Then I can talk about Henry and see what sort of reaction I get; see how she feels about him." I rubbed Buddy's ears some more and he pressed his head into my hand.

I reached inside and got his leash. We headed toward the front of the park and the itinerant section. No luck – she was gone again.

CHAPTER 11

JUSTINE

I was knitting on the porch when I heard a vehicle door slam loud enough that it sounded like a gunshot. Immediately the Jaxsons' birds erupted into a cacophony of objection.

I peeked over my truck and then checked with my tongue to see if my teeth were in. Then I ducked back into the trailer to grab Buddy's leash, my trash and my teeth.

There was a silver Mercedes parked behind Henry's SUV. The purple-haired woman slammed through the porch door and yelled at the birds. She disappeared inside and then came back out with her phone to her ear.

"I'm here. Where are you?"

A murmur came from the phone.

"You just left the birds here alone with the door unlocked? They're expensive birds, you know! Where's my mother?"

Another pause.

"Of course, they called and told me! I just don't know where it is." She listened a few more seconds and then apparently hung up on someone – I assumed Ralph.

"You there!"

I raised my eyebrows at her tone.

"Do you know where they took my mother?"

My first reaction was to be as bitingly rude as she was. Trust me, I could do that. "Honey," I repeated to myself in Albert's voice, "honey gets better results." Aloud, "I presume you are Jessica's daughter?"

"I would think that was bloody obvious, don't you?"

"You don't look anything alike. She has red hair." I smiled sweetly.

She looked like she was going to explode but then realized the absurdity of the statement. Jessica's hair should have been stark white but was a brilliant red.

Her own hair was an improbable shade of lavender. She laughed.

"That's better." I said. "I don't know where she's been taken, but I can give you the Sheriff's number and they can tell you, and also tell you how to go about getting access to her, or how to get her out. I'm sure she is under lock and key."

"They implied as much. I haven't actually talked to my mother in quite some time. Is she really as bad as they are saying?"

"I don't know what anyone has told you, but she can't be left alone. She can't take care of herself; eating for an example. She gets lost if she gets out of sight of the trailer. She doesn't recognize anyone or talk to friends anymore."

"I just looked at the house. It's a mess and I can't stay here."

"I'm sure Henry was trying to keep up with it. It's hard to keep up with housework when you are the only caregiver to someone as demanding as Jessica could be." I defended him.

"I don't know anything about these birds, either." She complained with distaste.

"You may have just burned your bridges with Ralph as far as taking care of them." I pointed out carefully. "But you can ask Lucy. She lives here in the park and babysat the birds when they left town last week. She took them to her own trailer but she may agree to come up here every day if you want her to."

"I'll call Mr. Emerson back, first. I was perhaps a little short and should apologize. Maybe he'll forgive the tantrum."

She eyed me again. "What do you know about all of this? Where has that ne'er-do-well husband of hers gone to? Have they found him or his body yet?"

"Not that I'm aware of; but I'm just a neighbor you know. Not really entitled to any inside information. Do you need the S.O.'s number?" I was a little shocked at her prompt assumption that a body would be involved.

"I have it."

She dismissed me without another word, picking a number out of her phone and relegating me and my dog to the scenery.

Buddy and I continued on to the dumpster and detoured the long way back past where Lucy lived with Jesus. Her vehicle was gone again. I would have to come back later to snoop.

Nathan was coming back from walking Angie and we met up at the mouth of the cul-de-sac.

"Jessica's daughter Justine is here." I nodded toward the quiet trailer.

"I know. I heard her talking to you. That was why I didn't come out. She is not a very nice woman." Nathan looked at me sideways.

"I hadn't noticed!" I lied cheerfully.

"If you didn't it's because you can be that way, too!"

"Now, Nathan. Surely you can't mean that!"

We were both laughing when we separated at my porch.

I called Cheyanne. "Are you going to Bingo with me? I was supposed to sit with Martha's bunch, two weeks ago. Do you suppose the offer is still good?"

"I suppose I can go. You'll have to show me the ropes, I haven't played since I was a child."

"No similarity at all. Just bring a snack of some kind, I'm bringing cheese and crackers."

"Okay."

Sally was selling the cards (which are no longer cards but sheets of paper specially printed for the semi-professional

Bingo crowd) and I had already purchased two ink daubers from a discount store so we each had one to use.

The program had barely launched when a man bustled into the room and up to his wife.

The caller was miffed and stopped the game. There were boos and hisses from the previously "ruly" crowd, now becoming "unruly."

"Well?" Demanded Martha, impatiently. "What is so all-fired important that it couldn't wait?"

"The Sheriff's Office started searching for Henry a couple of hours ago and found him in the woods to the west of the park." The informant held his breath for a dramatic pause. "Dead."

I looked down at the sheet I had been slowly completing. The red splotches on the light blue numbers now reminded me of bloody fingerprints.

Pandemonium broke out.

CHAPTER 12

WHO DONE IT?

It was our usual caucus on my porch. Cheyanne, Albert and Rose Marie, and I, discussing the Bingo game of the night before. Notice I said Bingo game, singular. There was only the one.

I thought the reasonable reaction to the news would have been to cancel the evening right then. However, the Bingo ladies take Bingo very seriously.

Consequently, that game was played to completion. I don't even know who won. I have to admit I stayed to the end of the game, though, just to see what would happen next.

When an anonymous "bingo" came from the back row it was announced that Bingo would resume the next evening to finish the remaining twelve games.

There was immediate protest. The loudest was "We have Bible study on Wednesday night."

That particular excuse was considered valid because it was being held forth by easily half the participants.

The games were then adjourned to Thursday night. Same bat time, same bat place.

Gossip had started immediately. It was absolutely amazing the number of gospel truths that were held forth from the little bit of real information they had gotten.

Suddenly everyone knew how he had died. They didn't. Suddenly everyone knew what he was doing in the woods. They didn't. Suddenly it was murder and everyone knew who did it. Jessica's daughter.

Somehow, and with no surprise, Justine had managed to alienate everyone in the park with the same ease with which she breathed.

She had been rude to a Good Samaritan, Ralph. She had been rude to a protected young member of the community, Lucy. She had been accusatory toward the respected manager, Jeremiah. She was dismissive and unconcerned about her mother. Lastly, she had been abusive toward a well-liked, deceased (and thereby imbued with saintly qualities) resident, Henry.

It was only in our own small company that I pointed out quite reasonably that as much as I would love to blame her, she hadn't even shown up until well after Henry's disappearance.

Not my problem, this time. I was not going to get involved.

CHAPTER 13

ROOMMATE

"Have you been over to the crime scene?" I asked Rose Marie. I kept one eye on Albert. He knew he was included in the question even if Rose didn't know he was there.

Albert shook his head.

"Why would I?" She was honestly shocked at my question.

"Well, you feed the cats back there somewhere. I just thought you might have seen the activity."

"Actually, I did see the commotion. It was near to where I feed them, but closer to the graveyard."

"Graveyard?" Eyebrows; mine, Cheyanne's and Albert's shot up.

"Animals don't live forever, or even very long, sometimes. I can't afford to have them cremated, so I bury them near the abandoned single-wide trailer at the far edge of the property next door."

She continued defensively, "Jeremiah knows. He owns about twenty acres of the woods next door. I do his mending and he ignores that I feed the cats and bury small animals on his property."

"They actually found Henry between where I feed them and where I bury them."

"What would Henry be doing back there?" I pondered.

"Not your problem, Patty!" Rose Marie interjected. "You don't want to get involved again, remember?"

I laughed, she was, after all, just quoting me.

Cheyanne actually looked like she did want to be involved.

Albert just shook his head.

"Actually, it was Jeremiah who suggested that I feed the cats over there. Last year when they were trying to evict me for having too many cats, he offered me the trailer for the purpose. It was too far away to be practical for me, though."

Rose Marie looked like she had forgotten any of us were even there; she was just talking to herself.

"I have seen Henry back there every once in a while, usually late in the evening or very early in the morning. I figured he was just taking a secluded walk while Jessica was asleep. Once in a while I would offer him a pastry or a cup of coffee."

"He just needed to talk, damn it! He was a very nice man, even if he wasn't very bright." Rose pointed out. "I was happy to just let him talk once in a while."

Apparently, she was winding down. She was running out of revelations and declarations. She shook the oak leaves off her skirt when she stood up to go.

It was easy to tell how much this all had affected her.

Random leaves rain down on whoever sits on my porch. Squirrels and birds cause them to fall on the unsuspecting guests. Buddy has long become accustomed to them and even ignores the random acorn that lands on his head.

She turned to go, still in her own little world until she got to the edge of the concrete. There she remembered her manners and turned to wave good bye. "I have to go fix up a basket of goodies for Ralph and his wife. He took pity on the birds and is caring for them again."

As Rose disappeared around the corner, the Mercedes pulled back in behind Henry's, I mean Jessica's, SUV.

We stared at the daughter with curiosity, didn't even pretend not to. She was the spectacle of the week. She saw us looking at her and marched over.

"I remember you." She glanced at me and then turned her attention to Cheyanne. "I don't know you, however. I'm Justine Smithers. I'm looking for an empty camper-trailer. The manager gave me a phone number for a young woman who owns a trailer back here and she has agreed to rent it to me for a month."

She looked around in faint distaste.

"You're not staying with Jessica in her house?" Cheyanne asked in surprise. "I'm Cheyanne, it's nice to meet you."

"My mother will not be returning to that home. She needs far more care than I will be able to provide. She will be placed somewhere suitable. I am here to settle her affairs. I can't live in that – space - with those birds. Besides, it needs a very thorough cleaning."

"Or a match." Her rant had left us both in shock. She looked uncomfortable that we hadn't gotten up, agreed with her, or made any polite offers.

"Would you like some grape Kool-Aid?" I offered. On second thought, she might not be old enough to remember Reverend Jim Jones.

"Oops, I meant root beer Kool-Aid." I kept a straight face even as I thought Albert was going to fall off his perch. Cheyanne was confused at Albert's response. I would have to explain later.

"You're putting her in an institution?" I asked, just to clarify the situation.

"Do I detect censure? You must have never had to care for anyone twenty-four-seven. I just need to know which camper these keys go to."

Both Albert and Cheyanne knew my story. I had been caregiver for both my last two husbands. If anyone knew about long-term caregiving, it was me.

They held their breath (at least Cheyanne did and Albert would have if he could have) and looked at me to see what I would do.

I stood up and told Justine Smithers she was free to find the camper on her own, or get lost on her own, but I never wanted to see her face again.

She looked at Cheyanne for explanation but was met with a stormy glare. She turned on her heel and marched back to her vehicle. She was going to get Jeremiah, or maybe Pete, to show her where she was going to stay.

I was shaking with fury until I turned and caught the look on Albert's face.

Of course.

Albert's daughter was renting out his camper to that awful woman. She hadn't decided what to do with it yet and decided to make a quick buck on it in the meantime.

Albert was being displaced.

His face registered horror at his new roommate.

CHAPTER 14

FAMILY TIES

"You can stay here, of course." I put in quickly.

Cheyanne made her own offer. "I have lots of room, three bedrooms. One is an office, but the other is an empty guest room you are welcome to." She looked at him with sympathy.

"I suppose I knew the day would come when it wouldn't be mine anymore, but I had kind of hoped I would be gone by then." He shook his head. "Share with her?"

All practicality, I pointed out that we'd better hurry if there was anything in there he wanted before she came back. "We can use the spare key and get anything you want out now. We can store it here and move it to Cheyanne's later. I gestured for them to follow me quickly.

He looked at us sadly as Cheyanne stood to join me in my recovery mission. "There really isn't, I guess. At one time there would have been a picture of Muriel. Forget that. There there's a picture of my daughter and I, but she hasn't even bothered to come down. Nothing about me was important to her, so why should she be important to me? You two are closer to me than anyone else in the world."

He smiled at us. "My new family."

"I can't watch the DVDs or listen to the CDs, or even read my books."

"Thank you, Patty for inviting me to stay with you. I know it was heartfelt, but I also know how much space you have and I would drive you nuts in a heartbeat."

He continued as he looked at Cheyanne. His gratitude was, at best, dispirited, but she knew it had nothing to do with her. "Thank you, Cheyanne. I will take you up on your offer for when I am not either here, with Dahlia, or in the other world."

He stood. "Lead on, McDuff."

The two of them headed off to inspect his new space and to undoubtedly negotiate terms similar to his and mine to help them get along.

Albert paced himself to her slower pace, his shoulders slightly slumped.

I wanted to cry. Cheyanne looked back and said she'd see me at Bingo later.

No sooner than they disappeared around my fence than Pete pulled up with his golf cart and the Mercedes following him.

He indicated where she should park. This was only about ten feet from where she had already been parking. She looked at the grass and weed patch and promptly returned her vehicle to the relative security of Jessica's carport. She picked her way across the rip-rap in her heels and I hoped she would turn an ankle.

Pete looked at me curiously and I wondered what she had told them up in the office about her reception here. I un-chained Buddy and took him inside, slamming my door for good measure.

I took my teeth out. I wanted nothing more to do with the outside world the rest of the day.

Oh, yeah. Bingo. Well at least for the rest of the afternoon.

Jessica was probably better off in even a halfway decent facility than relying on the care and kindness of her daughter, anyway.

I wondered what would happen to the birds.

I got online and found a bird rescue, tropical, parrots. Just in case someone should ask, I wrote down the contact information. I could give it to Ralph. I know he cared for the birds, but doubted he and his wife were in a position to commit to forever care for two birds likely to live past eighty years old.

I eventually took Ashes outside and put her in the little wire crate on the porch – her outside safe house. I re-chained Buddy and settled on the porch with a book of crossword puzzles. I couldn't stay cooped up inside for long; especially when the weather was that great.

I was out there staring at a twelve-space word that started with an "R" – unwilling or stubborn. Patty can be unwilling and stubborn, but only has five letters and doesn't start with an "R." Rose Marie started with an "R" but only has ten letters – counting the space.

What could I take for a snack tonight? Roquefort. Only nine letters and not even remotely the definition. I was getting farther away and not paying any attention to the puzzle. I tossed the book aside and startled my poor little cat.

A sheriff's vehicle pulled into the space by Albert's camper. He knew which one it was because he had responded when Albert died.

I wondered if they had told that awful woman why it was empty, but still stocked with canned and packaged food. I had cleaned up when Albert asked me to, but I think he was the only one who knew I had – it wasn't official or at his daughter's request. For all they knew it was still a mess.

The deputy looked right and left. He had expected a vehicle to be where he parked, Justine's Mercedes. He hadn't even looked at the carport next door, why should he?

Then he saw me and headed in my direction.

"She's there. She's just too good to park on sand. Her vehicle is at her mother's." I turned my back on him and went back inside, leaving my animals to guard my flank.

I heard him knock on her door and heard him ask if she would come out and talk to him. There was PVC furniture on the porch, four chairs and a glass top table, but they had been out all winter and were dirty.

She looked in distaste at the seating and invited him in instead. Albert's trailer was slightly bigger than mine and arranged differently. He had a couch and a chair. Two people could sit and talk without being engaged to be married.

I was back outside. Buddy and I needed a walk. We set off and then I went back after my teeth. I was getting better about wearing them but...

I carried crackers and guacamole to Bingo that night. The hall was noisy and crowded with more than the usual players. They had shown up, presumably, to gossip.

That wouldn't last long. Bingo was deadly serious to some of these folks. (Did I really just say that?) Talkers would be tossed out on their ears. I figured since we had already played the first game, guests might be allowed to stay maybe a quarter of an hour.

I sat down and looked for Cheyanne. She entered with a plate of cheese and olives wrapped in lunchmeat with a toothpick. It was pretty.

She settled next to me and looked at my equipment. “I forgot to ask, before. Where do you get those dauber things?”

“Sally has them for sale at an inflated price, but you can get them at any drugstore or discount mart. You’ve seen them, you just weren’t looking for them before.”

“What do you know about what happened to Henry?”

“Why should I know?” I set my jaw stubbornly. “Not my problem."

“Think what a good story it will make!” She exclaimed. “You have to figure it out!”

“I hate to point this out but I can make it a great story without knowing anything."

"I would probably make Ralph the culprit just because he was best friends with Henry. The great thing about writing is that I can make up facts and details and end it any way I want to."

She was disappointed in me, I could tell, partly because I was grouchy, partly because she knew I really was interested.

"Besides, I pretty much cut off any avenue of information when I ran Justine off my patio."

She grinned at the memory. "I could help. I hear she is looking for someone to clean out the mobile home so she can sell it. She's having a little trouble finding someone. I could volunteer, make some money and snoop at the same time. Lucy or Rose Marie might help me."

"She knows we're friends."

"Beggars can't be choosers."

"THIS BINGO SESSION IS ABOUT TO COMMENCE!" Once Sally had our attention she continued in a more reasonable voice. "All non-participating parties should leave to avoid being a distraction."

There was an exodus.

During the intermission later, we nibbled on the various snacks people had brought. A mousy woman with a pretty face (I had no idea who she was) came over and asked me who killed Henry.

"Someone said I should ask Potato Woman and pointed you out." She shivered. "We're all scared and locking our doors at night, now."

"I really don't have any idea who killed Henry, or even if it was murder, for sure." I just shook my head at my reputation having morphed into that of a psychic.

She was disappointed, but it must have been just idle curiosity on her part because she then jumped to the next question. "Why do they call you Potato Woman?"

I scowled at her. "I don't know that, either."

Cheyanne just laughed as the pretty mouse scurried off.

CHAPTER 15

DETECTIVE BOATRIGHT

Detective Boatright sat on my glider and sipped root beer Kool-Aid. We had come a long way since I first moved in here.

"Potato Woman? Nancy Drew or Agatha Christy, I could understand. It took me a while to figure out it was you they told me to talk to." He raised his eyebrows in query, and humor accentuated the crinkles around his eyes.

"Believe me, I have no idea and no one will tell me where the name started. I don't even know who *they* are. Who sent you to me?" I grimaced. "That makes it even worse. Maybe you can ask a few people while you're investigating Henry's death." I sipped Kool-Aid from my pickle jar. "Admit it. You would have come to me sooner or later, anyway."

He just grinned at me.

"By the way, I'm assuming you are here because he didn't just have a heart attack while running away from a bear or something."

"No. It was more violent than that. Where were you Sunday morning?"

I thought back. "What time?"

"Humor me and start at the beginning and tell me everything."

I left out Albert's presence at my pancake and egg breakfast. "Then I took Buddy for a walk down to the end of the road and back. That took maybe forty-five minutes. I wound up at Rose Marie's at seven-thirty or seven-forty-five. We walked over to Cheyanne's with various gardening implements to make her yard acceptable to the tenants' association. We finished about noon-thirty and Cheyanne and I came back here for Kool-Aid. We visited for an hour or so. Cheyanne went home. Buddy and I went to the store after sushi for the birthday party."

"Rose doesn't go to park functions, so Cheyanne and I met up a few minutes early and walked to the clubhouse."

He had been scribbling notes. "Noon-thirty?"

"Tell me that's not self-explanatory!" I gave him a disgusted look. "I worked on a twenty-four-hour clock for a very long time."

"The three of you were together the whole time you were doing yard work?"

"Well, Cheyanne went inside once to get us water and I went inside once to use the bathroom. What time did Henry die?" After all, I was answering questions, it was my turn to ask a few.

He just laughed at me. "I'm sure you'll figure it out eventually, after you re-interview everyone I do."

"Not me. I'm just curious. Besides, that witch Jessica spawned doesn't like me, why should I do her any favors?"

"What about for Mrs. Jaxson?" He asked gently.

He had hit a soft spot.

"She probably doesn't even really know he's permanently gone. Doesn't she pretty much live in the moment, now?" I protested weakly.

"She keeps referring to jewelry that is missing. One minute she says it was stolen and the next she claims Henry gave it to "that woman." She accuses her daughter of conspiring to kill her with "that man" who takes care of the birds. She talks about an insurance policy." He shook his head a little. "I can repeat all of this because I have heard her shout it in her room for all the world to hear. What can you tell me about any of that?"

"Well, if she had jewelry, I never saw it. But this is not exactly a formal kind of atmosphere, here. Her daughter would probably be the only one to know anything about family pieces."

"Henry didn't have time to be involved with anyone else. Rose said he was lonely and worn out, she gave him coffee or a donut every so often when he was going past on a walk." I pet Buddy while I thought. A squirrel bounced on a branch over the neighbor's roof and falling acorns made a resultant clatter.

"Why was he in the woods?" I tried again for an answer of some kind.

"You tell me..." He responded.

"Thanks for nothing," I commented.

"Ralph was Henry's best friend and seemed to get along with Jessica okay, from what anyone else can tell. They all sat outside on the porch a lot, companionably. Ralph is not a huge fan of the daughter. Besides, he had to get Jessica to cough up a notebook of phone numbers so he could call Justine the other day when I was there. If there had been a conspiracy, he would have had her number."

The detective made notes of some kind in his own notebook.

"As for insurance, Henry would have been smart to insure her, but it would have to be an old policy – I doubt if she has been insurable for quite some time." I continued. "Besides that, what would a policy on her have to do with killing Henry?"

"Why doesn't Rose Marie go to park functions?"

"Because the narrow-minded few who run things here have anyone who is not narrow-minded, too cowed to buck them. They are jealous of her."

"Well that was as clear as mud."

“Who found Henry?” I asked.

“One of the deputies who was looking for him. There’s a trail from Rose Marie’s trailer back into the woods; why?”

“She feeds the feral cat population back there. She is only allowed to have two cats here in the park.” I defended her.

“Was he killed in the woods or was he killed somewhere else and dumped there?”

“Thank you.” He ignored me. “I’m sure we’ll be talking again soon.”

He had gotten far more from me than I had from him, but it was a start. Next time would be my turn.

CHAPTER 16

TIME OF DEATH

"I heard Detective Boatright on the radio. The time of death was between eight and noon on Sunday morning." Albert supplied more details later in the day. "He also talked to Ralph, Rose Marie and Cheyanne. He had his men go through Jessica's mobile home. Justine had found a policy on Henry, but not on Jessica. It was for a cool two hundred and fifty thousand. Jessica was the beneficiary, naturally. At least she will be able to afford good care for the rest of her life."

"Did they find any jewelry?" I pumped him shamelessly.

"I heard the daughter describing some family pieces that were apparently quite valuable. They were looking for the murder weapon in the woods but couldn't find anything."

Rose Marie came around the corner carrying an old-fashioned basket with a cloth covering the contents. "Hi, Patty. I need a friend and I come bearing gifts."

"Welcome! And not just because you are bearing what I am reasonably sure are baked goods; judging from Buddy's reaction." Buddy was bouncing like a puppy begging and excited to see her.

"Bring me some water and I'll just set these out here. I brought extras for you to share with Nathan or whomever if you want."

Settled comfortably, she sighed. "Detective Boatright just left. Someone told him Henry and I were friends and then he got a definition of "friends" from Martha." She grinned wryly. "Now he is convinced we were having a torrid affair."

"It's a good thing I was working with you and Cheyanne all morning." She continued. "Otherwise I suspect I would be in big trouble."

"His estimated time-of-death was in the morning." I bit my lip and then had to admit it to her. "I told him you had coffee with him once in a while. I'm sorry. I actually was telling him that a cup of coffee with someone once in a while was all Henry had time for. I didn't realize he would take it differently."

Rose Marie eyed me closely for a minute. "Martha is probably the one who first put that spin on it. But you certainly didn't do me any favor."

"You have a firm alibi for the time of death."

"What could he have been doing back there so early that morning? That's when Ralph saw him. Jessica was, from all accounts, alone all day from then on. Henry used to go for walks, but he was never gone that long." Rose Marie scratched Buddy's ears and he lay his head on her foot in ecstasy.

"I may have to get a lawyer. I'm used to being blamed for things around here, but murder is different. There's a lawyer I know from the grocery store every once in a while. He bakes, too." She got out her phone and looked to see if she had his number. She got up and took an apple fritter with her as she started to press the numbers for her baker/lawyer friend. She looked back at me. "Do me a favor and don't mention my name in any context whatever if that detective comes back, agreed?"

Shamefaced, I agreed. I really hadn't intended to cause her any trouble. She was the last person who would have hurt Henry.

My own phone rang shortly thereafter. I put down the blender, I was making dog food for Buddy (he had allergies) and wiped my hands off on the back of my shorts. "Patty." I answered impatiently.

"I have landed the cleaning job at the Jaxsons'. Lucy is going to help, but you had better keep your distance. So – since I have official permission to tear the house apart, what am I looking for?"

"Jewelry comes to mind, first. The murder weapon would be nice if we had any idea what it was. Evidence of anyone besides the Jaxsons, Ralph or Lucy might be important. Ralph was his best friend and Lucy was out of town."

I really had to do laundry or I was going to be running around naked. Potato Woman. Not a pretty picture.

It was two hundred steps to the laundry room if you stop at the dumpster first. I tied Buddy to the porch and sat on the bench to wait out the cycles. I needed to make notes.

CHAPTER 17

SEARCHING FOR WHAT?

Buddy and I went for a circuitous walk and came back past Dahlia's swing. She was standing by the tree looking towards Rose Marie's house. It was daylight and there were people around so I just nodded when she looked at us. Then I followed her gaze.

Rose Marie was standing in the road with a uniformed officer and there was a detective standing in the half-open door to an official vehicle.

She had her arms crossed and was pointedly not looking at the officer I could see now was there to keep her curbside, and out of the way.

Rose caught sight of us as Buddy pulled me closer. She gave a defiant look at the officer and turned her back on the whole bunch to walk over to me.

I raised an eyebrow in silent question.

With a disgusted look she indicated the Sheriff's car and the officers with a wave of her hand. "They haven't told me what they're looking for. They just waved a search warrant at me and told me to stay out here."

"Hey, you!" She called. "When the buzzer goes off on the oven, take the rolls out and turn it off, will you?"

She had her phone in her hand and held it up. "I called Mr. Brown. He said he would be here directly."

"There was another car, but when it was evident I wasn't going to get hysterical, they went to the "other site" wherever that is."

I stood silent in shock. How could they suspect Rose Marie? "Look, Rose, we're not supposed to know it, but you were with Cheyanne and I the whole time bracketed by the Medical Examiner. We already talked about that. I don't know what they would expect to find."

Then it occurred to me. "Jewelry? What would that have to do with the murder, though?"

She didn't answer, just looked partly angry and partly miserable.

"You're not still mad at me, are you?" I asked fearfully.

"No." There was a pause. "No. I'm not mad at you. Apparently, Jessica is telling people that Henry gave the jewelry to "that woman." There are any number of people in the park who consider me to be the only "that woman" around. So, they would have come back to me, anyway." Now she just looked sad and resigned.

I was glad I didn't live in her life. All the changes in emotion would be exhausting. I was tired just from trying to keep up with what she was feeling so I could react appropriately. Social cues had never been my forte and, although I had been doing better, lately, it was an effort.

A sleek, electric, black sedan pulled silently up and parked on the other side of the road just down from the cruiser so other vehicles could get past the circus going on here.

A tall, slender, bald man emerged from the vehicle with his long, black jacket flapping open around him. He looked like an insect emerging from a cocoon, but with a very attractive countenance; kind of like a cross between a praying mantis and Bruce Willis. Rose Marie brightened visibly and I realized this man in black was her Mr. Brown.

While I wouldn't have gone away and left her alone, I could go and leave her in this man's care, I knew. I hugged her and shook hands with the handsome black stranger. Buddy approved of him as well, and blessed him with a few golden hairs on his dark slacks. "You can come see me when they're done if you're up to it. Remember, you have nothing to worry about."

Buddy and I left and headed towards home. There was activity at the Jaxsons'. I recognized Cheyanne's vehicle, the hatch was open and she had cleaning supplies spilling out onto the ground in what looked like haphazard fashion. It was not; Cheyanne was nothing if not organized. She was parked on the grass because the Mercedes was in the driveway still behind the SUV. Ralph was inside talking to the birds and cleaning the cages. Lucy popped out with a broom and then a mop.

That reminded me. "Hey, Ralph. Have you found a home for the birds? I found a rescue place in St Augustine that will probably take them."

He peered through the screen at me. "I talked to them a couple of days ago." He looked quickly behind him to see who was listening. "That witch refused to let them take them. She said they were worth a fortune and she was going to sell them. Then she asked me to help and I refused." He explained. "You can't do that to them. They shouldn't be separated, and most people don't have a clue how to take care of them or what an enormous responsibility they are. She tried the pet shop who also referred her to the rescue people and she finally gave in."

He paused to pour water. "They are on their way now. I'm packing up everything to go with them. I know she's planning on selling everything separately because I saw a list of things she planned on getting rid of and what she thought she could get for them. I hope they get here soon, before she stops me. These birds need their things around them more than she needs the few hundred their things might bring."

"Justine was really pleased about the life insurance policy she found in Jessica's purse, though."

"What an odd place to keep an insurance policy." I commented.

"Yeah, well, you know Jessica, paranoid to the max." He hesitated. "She apparently had cash, receipts, the titles to the trailer and the SUV and Lord knows what all in her purse to keep safe. I saw Justine rooting through them. She got really angry about some of the receipts she found."

He stood on a bench and took down several chains holding bird swings. He gathered them up and put them in a box. He plucked a few feathers from the chains and from the wooden parts. He frowned at one. Then he coaxed the birds onto the top of the cages and was looking at their feet. He was smoothing their feathers and talking to them softly. One rubbed his head on Ralph's wrist.

"They have been really upset at both Henry and Jessica for being gone from them so long. Jasper has been pulling out feathers." He showed me a bare patch on one of the birds.

Cheyanne came bustling out and saw me. "Can't you yell "fire" or something so this woman will run away and leave us alone?" She whispered through the screen, then came out to the road. The knees of her jeans were wet and there were smudges on her arms.

"I gather there was never anyone else but Henry and Jessica in the trailer. Even Ralph and Lucy were usually just on the porch or maybe the kitchen." She wiped her hands on a towel she had tucked in her waistband.

"It's a pity how some older folks fall through the cracks. They lived, as far as I can tell, on frozen dinners and I'm sure

Henry was just too overwhelmed to even try to keep things clean. It's pretty bad."

"I suppose the children are normally the resource who would notice the problem and take up the slack. Obviously, Mrs. Mercedes, here, was not a resource. His kids? We don't know anything about them."

"I gather the only number they had for his son was disconnected. The officers are looking for him since witch-woman wouldn't." She turned to go back in.

"I'd better get back before Lucy thinks I've abandoned her. You had better disappear."

Rose Marie showed up late that afternoon. She looked absolutely wrung out. I got her a glass of the wine I keep for emergencies (and cooking). It was red; she grimaced.

"Sorry. I only keep red because I don't have to chill it."

"Since when do you drink wine?" She asked absently as she admired the pretty color in the pickle jar/wine glass.

"I really don't. I've been designated driver for so long it doesn't even occur to me to drink anything."

"You don't happen to have a rolling pin I can borrow, do you?"

I laughed. "Of course, I do! What kind of cook would I be without one?"

"One being indicted for murder."

That cut my laugh off short and I poured myself a jar of wine as well.

"Tell me."

"They started looking in the kitchen for a rolling pin. They found one and seemed to be satisfied until someone realized there was another one behind it and then a third. One was good, but more than one was bad because if there were four there might have been five. I had to explain ad-nauseum why I had four. One was marble. One was patterned. That, they finally understood, but why two plain wooden ones?"

"One was your mother's?"

"Grandmother's." She agreed and explained at the same time.

"That was only the start. Finding the rolling pins was easy. Then they turned the house upside down and inside out looking for the jewelry." She sipped again and made another face.

"Would you rather have something else?"

"No. This is fine, thank you. They even dumped the flour, sugar and cornmeal into bowls and sifted them. They emptied every box in the pantry that had been opened. Fortunately, most everything in the freezer was in original containers or in clear plastic wrap.

"They even went through the plastic grocery store bags." She frowned. "They took the receipt they found in one. I usually leave them in the bags since they're going to be for trash anyway."

"I'm not sure why one of them would be significant."

"Wow. Thorough."

"I do have to admit. They were really pretty neat. I mean you see houses on television that are completely trashed by searchers. The deputy assigned to keep me out of trouble and out of the way said they really had doubts about me, they had absolutely no motive whatever. She probably shouldn't have told me that, so don't repeat it."

I raised my hand. "Scout's honor. I guess that makes it pretty clear they think the murder weapon was a rolling pin."

"I know it's sexist, but that also points toward its being a woman, too, right?" She held out her jar for more of the wine.

"I was about to agree with you until I thought about your lawyer being a baker." I retorted as I returned with her jar and brought the rest of the bottle out with me. I also gave Buddy a treat out of my pocket.

"Touché."

"And, since I brought the subject up, tell me more about your lawyer. Don't tell me you aren't closer than just bakery-aisle-buddies! I thought you weren't interested anymore?"

She blushed. "Just friends. Let it go for a while. After this is over, we can talk about him."

CHAPTER 18

THE WOODS

Albert teased me for not being at the generic church service at the clubhouse, again.

I didn't bother to answer since we had already discussed that to death. "So, you were scarce yesterday. What were you up to?"

"I hung out with the girls while they were cleaning for most of the day."

"You do know that Cheyanne is roughly the same age as me – why is she a girl and I am Potato Woman?"

"Are you going to keep interrupting me with your petty jealousy?"

"I am not." I was, actually, just a little. I didn't see as much of him since Cheyanne came around and he moved into her guest room.

"Ralph was there until the bird people came for the parrots. It's a good thing the daughter had to leave before they got there, because he gave them lock, stock and barrel – big cages, little cages, toys, food, perches and swings."

"I'll bet she was livid when she got back. Where did she have to go?"

"She went to the facility where her mother is."

"I'm surprised she would go visit – I'd have bet Jessica would never see her again."

"I don't think she had a choice. The administrator called and summoned her; something about a private room." He grinned at Patty. "The girls made sure they were done and gone before she got back."

It was Sunday and Rose Marie's day off. I gathered up Buddy and his leash and he leapt down the steps to pay a visit to our friend.

"Are you busy? I took a chance; we haven't seen a lot of you the last few days."

"I have bread raising, but I only just covered it so I have an hour. What do you have in mind?"

"Can we go for a walk? I'd like to see where you feed the cats, the cemetery and the old trailer. It would make it easier to see it in my mind."

"So, you can put it all in your next book?" She teased, "after all, you have no interest in the current mystery, or in the crime scene."

"Exactly!" I agreed.

She slipped on her crocs and led me to a small path through the undergrowth.

Buddy hung back and looked at me with reproach. "I know. You're a house dog. Just this once, today, please Big Guy?"

With a very human sigh, he followed me. He was the first one to see a cat and brightened up considerably.

“I don’t usually come back here during the day, so they are probably mostly off somewhere else until tomorrow morning at feeding time.” With that she brushed back an elephant ear leaf and we were in a small clearing. A stump and a fallen log supported several small dishes, all licked clean.

“Where do you keep the food?”

“I tried keeping it back here, even in a metal trash can with a lid, but the critters invariably got into it. Raccoons. Once it was a bear. Now I carry it back in a pitcher. In the rain I put the bowls under the palmettos.”

She led me farther across the clearing and down another faint trail. "This way to the cemetery."

Buddy and I hustled along to keep up.

We passed a place with orange tape staked around it, marked "Do Not Enter" every few feet. Farther to the south, there was a spot where numerous vehicles had entered and parked, no doubt supporting the investigation? There was an outline in the dirt in the circle. I didn't see any blood. Maybe they collected it all?

We stood briefly, but there was really nothing left to see, so we skirted the area and went on.

The first thing I saw was a six-foot chain-link fence overgrown with weeds. I was sure that must be where the trailer was, but it was so overgrown you couldn't actually see it. Then I saw the rows of neat wooden crosses. Rose had very neatly buried and marked the graves of almost a dozen small animals. Even Buddy sat down quietly. I reached over for Rose Marie's hand and gave it a squeeze. "This is so very nice. You've done a nice job for them."

"Do you want to see the trailer?" Rose Marie turned her head to hide her eyes and led the way around the corner of the fence. "This is one of those Florida things. By the path we followed, it is really pretty close to the park, but it's a lot easier to reach by the road, even if it is three miles that way."

There was a gate and a driveway on the far side of the property. There was a shiny new padlock on the gate.

“I guess I don’t want to see it today!”

"That didn't used to be on there. I wonder when Jeremiah did that?"

We made it back to the rising bread before her timer went off. I sniffed. “Raisin? Enough for me?”

Rose laughed. “Come back later.”

Buddy and I walked home the long way, just because Buddy wanted to. I thought about Rose’s rolling pin.

I suddenly remembered where I had seen another one recently.

The bird swing on the Jaxsons’ porch. Held by two chains it hung from their ceiling. I saw in my head as Ralph looked at it and hung it back up that Sunday afternoon. Then I remembered him carefully including it in everything he conveniently sent way out of town with the bird rescue people.

Was he including it less out of compassion and more to get rid of evidence? Could the time of death be off a little? Could Ralph have hit him, taken the rolling pin back to the house and managed to make it to breakfast with his friends, his alibi? It had seemed pretty solid alibi when added to the absolutely no motive thing.

I was back to motive. Why?

I could hear a loud voice as Buddy and I turned toward home.

"What do you mean you can't accept the claim until the homicide is solved?"

Pause.

"How could my mother possibly be guilty? She's locked up for being incompetent. You can't credit anything she says or does."

Pause.

"She couldn't be found guilty of murder, anyway. She has Alzheimer's."

Pause.

"I don't believe that. That's ridiculous." She stuck the phone in her pocket, having hung up on still another person.

"It was that Ralph person who did it anyway." She spat out in my direction – apparently needing an audience.

Convenient now that you don't need him to take care of the birds. I couldn't say it out loud, though, especially in light of my own thoughts, moments ago.

She glared at me. "I suppose *I'll* have to prove it just so that insurance company will settle. They're stalling because they don't want me to have the money. It's ridiculous. They claim Alzheimer's isn't an insanity defense and she could be charged."

"Does the Sheriff's Department really think she could have followed him into the woods and hit him, then come back, hid the weapon, and then pretended to not know anything?"

Justine was ranting to herself, not to me. Once again, I was just part of the scenery.

I melted away with my Buddy.

CHAPTER 19

JESSICA'S TEMPER

"It might be silly, but I really miss those birds." I sipped a smoothie made of mincemeat, (fruit is good for you) milk, and peanut butter for protein. Good stuff. Better than Kale.

"Do you have any idea how many calories are in that?" Albert asked me.

"Don't know. Don't care." I took another sip and sighed. "Don't tell me."

Then I finished it. "Don't tell Cheyanne, either. I told her I was on a smoothie diet to lose weight."

He looked hurt. "Of course not."

"It's not that it's quiet without the birds, but they added a whole additional layer of sound. I can't believe how many birds are here even without them. Why would a bird live somewhere cold and snowy without anything to eat? They should all come here."

"Goodness. Are you turning into a birder?"

"Whatever that is. No. The Audubon Society is safe from me." I looked down where Buddy was laying with his front paws splayed out in front of him and his ears perked toward some playing squirrels. "You should have seen him when we walked by and one of the birds would whistle or talk to him."

Buddy he knew he was the topic of conversation and pulled himself up to his feet – ever ready for a walk.

"Okay, big guy. Let me get my shoes and put my teeth in."

Albert just smiled and disappeared. Walking was too slow for him these days, he was spoiled.

We rounded the corner where there was a fence around the pool area and there was splashing. A lone figure pulled himself through the water steadily.

Ralph. Right, it was no-floatie time.

We watched until Buddy got restless; as soon as we started off Ralph climbed out of the shallow end, dripping and sopping the water out of his hair.

Good looking man, that Ralph, once I saw him almost in his all-together!

"Hey, Patty, Buddy."

It had been a while since anyone but the girls called me Patty – lately it was Potato Woman – I was startled. He came over to the fence and started toweling himself down. Then he wrapped the towel around his waist. It was blue with Spock's face on it and his hand making the sign for "Live Long and Prosper". Good choice, that.

"Good morning. Not a floatie in sight!" I commented.

He grimaced. "They're inside in a special storage area." He wiggled his fingers through the chain link and Buddy obligingly sniffed, hopeful that there was a treat even though he could probably only smell the chlorine.

He shared his plans for the day. "I'm going to go see Jessica today. I worry about her with no one but that witch looking out for her. I don't know who killed Henry; but I worry about her."

And I worry about her as well! Could Ralph be looking for a way to get rid of her even under the care of the nursing home?

Did he have a reason to? Did he have a reason to kill Henry?

"You know, I've been thinking about going to see her as well. Just a friendly face, you know. I was thinking about her this morning when I was missing the bird noise."

He looked surprised. "I didn't think you were friends with her."

"Not so much, but I regret that. I thought I would take her some of Rose's raisin bread. Like I said, a friendly face and all that. She probably needs all the friends she can get, right now." I winced inwardly at giving up any of Rose's bread.

Is he trying to talk me out of it?

"Would you like to go with me?" I was a little surprised, but then I realized I had backed him into a polite little southern corner.

"Thank you! That would be wonderful. What time should I be ready to go?"

"I'll meet you at the office at noon. I hate backing out of your cul-de-sac."

"Okay. Thank you!"

I turned to go back to the trailer and practically ran right through Albert. His face registered grave concern.

"Not here," I hissed.

He was waiting for me when we got back to my porch.

"What are you up to? I don't like you being alone with him. We don't know what happened, but it looks pretty bad for him, especially after the rolling-pin-thing."

"You can tell Cheyanne. I'll mention that she knows I'm going with him. He's not stupid."

"You can tell her yourself! She'll kill me if she knows I let you go!"

I just looked at him and he went back over what he had just said. He rolled his eyes as he realized why I was grinning.

We both laughed and he disappeared in a cloud of embarrassment.

Buddy was not happy at being left behind. His stubby little tail stayed firmly still as he tried to press past me out the door.

"You just went out. You have water. You ate a good breakfast, and you have the cat to play with."

He lowered his head to his paws and turned away from me to pout.

"Love you, Good Boy." I pulled the baby gate across the doorway to keep the cat in and then shut and locked the door. Albert joined me as I walked toward the office.

"Can't talk you out of it, can I?" He tried once more.

When we were in sight, I saw that the door to the office was shut. I could see Ralph and Jeremiah inside. They looked like they were arguing.

"I wonder what that's about," I mused.

Albert looked toward the office as well. "Stay here." He popped out.

I fretted and thought I looked conspicuous standing by the mailboxes way too early for the delivery. I pulled out my key and checked my box anyway.

“They’re arguing about some paper Henry had that they can’t find. They are also concerned that Ms. Smithers has all of Henry’s keys and something needs to be checked on.” He knew I was about to say something about him never eavesdropping. He held up his palm to stop me. "This was an exception."

The door to the office was yanked open and Ralph stormed out and headed for his car.

“Give him a minute to simmer down. You’re a little early, anyway,” Albert advised me cautiously. He looked at me again. "I still don't like this, you know."

I smiled at his paternal manner and would have tried to pat his hand if I could have. "I'll be good."

I meandered over and knocked on Ralph's passenger side window rather than just open his door.

He started, and then forced a smile. He reached over and opened the door from the inside.

"Thank you." I put the shopping tote with the bread on the floor and shoved it a little to one side with my foot as I clambered in. The car was low and a graceful entrance was out of the question. I hoped I could get out at the other end.

We drove with only a few remarks about weather on the way. We really had very little in common, after all. He finally added "I had to wait to see my wife off. She's going to visit her sister for a few days down in Sanibel."

"I've heard it's very nice down there."

"I thought about going with her," he admitted. But then he glanced at me. "Unfortunately, I really don't like her sister."

We both laughed, and any tension left dissipated.

A perky little twenty-something met us at the desk. "How can we help you?"

"We're here to visit Jessica Jaxson."

"Let me look her up."

I was a little disgusted. This place wasn't so big she shouldn't have known all the residents.

"I see here she is not available right now. Is there anything else we can do for you?"

"What do you mean not available? Is she at an appointment or something?"

"I'm sorry. We can't discuss her with anyone but her daughter. Is there anything else we can do for you?"

"If we came back, in, say, an hour?"

"You are always welcome to come back. We are here to be of service to the patients and their families."

"So, we could see her then," I interrupted the conversation between Ralph and Miss Perky. It was getting fishy.

"No. I'm sorry. She will be unavailable for visitors at that time."

Ralph and I exchanged looks. He looked about to explode all over her perky little desk. I shook my head slightly and led him a little way into the room stuffed with overstuffed chairs, stuffed pillows and stuffy magazines.

"Let's wait for a minute and see how things work here." There was a door stuffed in between two schefflera trees.

The wall was covered with tiny plaques naming donors to the facility. I wandered over to look at the names. Miss Perky ignored me, secure in her little locked world.

Another visitor came in and was buzzed through the door.

Another attendant with a matching blouse and bow took Miss Perky's place without looking around.

Another woman came in. She was using a walker and Ralph went out through the glass door and held it open for her. The bells on the door handle tinkled as he did so and Miss Replacement looked up. Ralph let the new guest approach the desk alone and rejoined me in the corner.

When Miss Replacement buzzed the door for the newcomer, Ralph opened it for her, and we followed her into the corridor.

She thanked us and we slipped silently down the hall reading the name plates on the doors as quickly as we could, looking purposeful and as if we belonged. We found a set of doors with windows in them (for observation?) with J Jaxson on them, and tried the door bar. It was locked.

We exchanged looks. The chance of getting through that door surreptitiously was about zero to none.

The little old lady we had helped made her way in our direction. She had simply traveled more slowly. "If you're trying to visit Mrs. Jaxson you're out of luck. She's been locked up since the incident."

"What incident?" We both asked.

"Come this way," instructed the little woman.

We followed her into a very pleasant room with big band music playing softly (as least as softly as big band music gets), green walls and blue appointments. There were tables with jigsaw puzzles, books, and magazines of all kinds. A huge flat screen television stood sentinel in one corner. We sat together on a couch when she chose a chair across from it. Ralph and I had gone from relative strangers to accomplices by sneaking in here.

"What incident?" I repeated.

"I'm Miss Robinson." She looked at me reproachfully for foregoing the mannerly lead-ins to the explanation.

Ralph had been raised in Florida and had, fortunately, better manners than I did. "It's nice to meet you, Miss Robinson."

"Gladys."

"Miss Gladys." He smiled at her.

"Much better. It's nice to have strangers to talk to. I can see, though, that you are concerned about your...?" She prompted for some give and take on our side.

I now understood the game a little better. “Aunt,” I supplied, “on my mother’s side. This is my husband, John. I’m Effie.”

So help me, she giggled. “You’re getting better but no one, and I mean no one, has been named Effie in the last hundred years.”

“Jessica turned violent a few days after she arrived. A male attendant took her dinner in to her and she threw it at him. She grabbed the tray and tried to bash him with it.”

“She followed him out past the nurse’s station, took a big stapler and hit him on the back of the head as they ran down the hall.”

"Jessica was screaming at him, calling him Henry, and yelling about some jewelry that was missing." Gladys was nodding her head to herself as she repeated the events to us.

"The Sheriff's Department came, and the word is that she will be charged with assault. The staff was angry that they hadn't been warned that she was aggressive."

Ralph responded with disbelief. "They can't charge her with assault. She's got Alzheimer's."

Miss Gladys was obviously pleased to set us straight. "No, sir. She can and will be charged. Alzheimer's patients are not considered insane and are not protected. Just a few years ago, one patient killed his roommate. He was 86, and he was convicted and sent to prison."

I sat, appalled, taking in all the implications while Ralph and Miss Gladys finished our game of manners with a few more platitudes and promises to see each other again. When he stood, I did as well, and finally focused on the sharp-eyed Miss Gladys again.

"Thank you, Ma'am." I leaned down and gave her a hug, and pressed the tote with the raisin bread into her lap.

We turned to walk out more sedately and without the stealth we had resorted to when we entered.

"Do you suppose Rose Marie has more of that bread?" Ralph asked in a stage whisper.

“I hope so!”

Miss Perky was back and narrowed her perky little eyes as she saw us emerge from the forested corner.

I smiled and gave her a little wave. Rub it in, rub it in.

When we were settled back in his car and halfway home, I finally mentioned the elephant in the back seat.

“You do realize, after hearing this, Jessica may have actually killed Henry.”

Ralph made a face. “I can’t see her following him into the woods and coming back. She got lost walking to the clubhouse, for crying out loud.” He sighed. “I didn’t kill him. I saw fuzz and what looked a little like blood on the rolling pin they used for a bird swing when I packed the bird stuff up to go."

I remembered him giving it a second glance when I was watching him pack. "That's why you were looking at the birds' feet? Looking for a cut or an injury?"

"Yes."

"The killer would have held it by the handle, using it as a weapon. I only remember you handling the roller part. If it comes down to it – point that out."

"I won't have to point that out if they don't know about the damn thing," he stated firmly.

"So, what do we do now?" I asked, half to myself.

He looked at me sideways. "We?"

I shrugged.

"I don't know. I need to think about it. There has to be someone else involved, in which case the rolling pin is irrelevant. I still can't see Jessica in the woods."

A picture of good old Jeremiah came to mind, but I couldn't admit I knew they had argued – about Henry?

CHAPTER 20

FRAUD

I thanked him for the ride and walked with my head down toward my trailer.

Buddy was howling. I wondered how long he had been doing that and looked around for angry neighbors.

Albert was at my shoulder as I unlocked the door; my good dog bounced out, headed for our small patch of grass to pee.

"He only started that when you got out of Ralph's car and he heard your voice."

I caught up with Buddy and fastened the porch chain to his collar. He was a good dog, yes, but I couldn't risk him running out in the road, much less climbing a tree. I pictured him up in the fork of the closest oak, his big paws on the branch and his eyes fixed on a chattering squirrel. I laughed.

Albert followed me into the trailer and waited for me to get a drink and lead him back outside.

"Jessica may well have killed Henry. I'm just not sure how."

Albert looked a little smug. "Deputy Boatright was back. He was in my trailer with Miss Witch."

"He told her that she needed to know, as Miss Jessica's guardian and closest relative, that Jessica could have been responsible for Henry's death. He was actually hit some time before he died. There was bleeding on the brain that built up until he collapsed, and then died shortly after – on that trail. He was on blood thinners – who isn't at his age?"

"Wasn't," he corrected himself automatically. "So, it took a while, but his blood didn't clot to stop it."

"The detective did admit that they still had another suspect, but in light of the incident at the nursing facility, and this new information, it didn't look good for her. She could have hit him before he left the house," Albert continued to report.

"Justine was furious. She said the insurance company was refusing to pay Jessica's claim, just in case she was guilty. They were spouting statistics about spouses."

"She did say the insurance company was paying the claim on the stolen jewelry, however."

We exchanged looks. We both read greed all over Justine's every action since she had arrived. We also knew from Pete that the jewelry pieces Henry had sold were probably the ones Justine was claiming to be gone. She would, after all, have control of any payout from the insurance companies.

"Didn't someone say something about Henry selling some jewelry? It wasn't stolen." I fretted. "I don't think Ralph did it."

"I don't either." Albert agreed.

"Don't what? Breathe? Eat? Zipline?" Cheyanne teased as she rounded the corner.

When Albert looked down sadly, she apologized. "I'm sorry Al. I was just teasing

– sometimes I put my foot in my mouth and I should really have kept quiet."

He smiled tremulously and accepted her apology with a nod. Buddy pushed his nose into Albert's hand and Albert patted him lightly and disappeared.

"Oh, dear. I didn't mean to upset him." Cheyanne's distress almost equaled his.

I brought her Kool-Aid and we settled on the porch. I caught her up to speed.

"Ralph could use a friend about now, I'm thinking." Cheyanne commented. "You say he's alone tonight? We could go and visit and take him some liquid comfort. Do you know what he drinks?"

"Albert says they all three used to drink beer on the porch."

"What kind? Does it matter? Doesn't all beer taste the same?" We laughed, the wine drinker and the tee-totaller.

"I'll go get some and we'll go after supper."

I avoided Albert the rest of the day by staying inside with the door shut. Something told me he would not approve of our plan. I hoped Cheyanne wouldn't share it with him.

She and I and Buddy traversed the park towards Ralph's home. I hadn't ever actually visited him, but kind of knew which one was his. I did know his vehicle...

There was a light on in the kitchen. We stopped at the door and called. There was no answer. The front door was locked.

It had been on the near side so we had gone to it first. Now we rounded the end of the trailer to the carport door. It was slightly ajar.

We called again and still got no response. “No one locks doors around here,” Cheyanne commented.

I smelled smoke. I pushed open the door and we went slowly into the kitchen. There was a pot on the stove with the melted remnant of a plastic lid smoldering on the bottom. The eggs had exploded and there were pieces of egg and shell on the ceiling, the floors, the walls, and trapped underneath the lid. It had popped up and flipped, melting its way down to burn on the bottom of the pot when it landed again.

Cheyanne and I looked at each other. She reached out to turn the burner off and move the pot. She pulled out her phone to call 911.

I didn't think there was time for that. Without explanation, Buddy and I slipped out the door and headed down the path that Henry had taken on that fateful morning. It was dark.

Why is it always dark when I'm in a hurry?

Buddy hurried behind me, stopping only once when he stepped on a thorn. I nearly pulled his collar over his head when he stopped abruptly. I knelt and used the flashlight on my phone to look. I pulled out the offending thorn and stroked his ears. "Good boy. Come on, now."

Bread crumbs? Lighted rocks? Solar stakes? Come on, come on, how did anyone expect me to find that place in the dark?

Easy answer. No one expected me to find that place in the dark.

I tripped once and now had dirt on my knees, sleeves, hands, and, probably, my face; just like the heroine in any B movie.

As we got closer to the trailer Henry had to have been heading for the day he died, I heard voices. I rounded the corner, saw the gate was open, and recognized Ralph's voice.

"I don't know what you thought you were going to find back here."

"Don't be stupid. You had to know Henry had a copy of your contract and I would find it."

"So, okay, you knew what was here. What was the point of marching me back here at gun point? Why not discuss it in my kitchen?"

I stopped and tied Buddy to the fence with his leash. Then I pulled out my phone and activated the recording function.

"You can't shoot me to prove your mother didn't do it. I would just be another dead body with no motive."

"I don't plan on shooting you, although your other partner would be a viable alternative to Mom. Business partners getting sideways of each other – happens all the time."

The voices were rising and falling as lights flicked on and off. She was apparently getting a tour.

"Well if you're not going to shoot me, why the gun?"

"I wanted to see for myself what was going on back here. They'll never convict my mother. I know what everyone is saying, but I don't believe a jury would convict her; and unless she is convicted, the insurance company will have to pay me."

Ralph agreed with her.

I would agree, too, if someone had a gun on me!

"So, let's celebrate our new partnership. I won't tell anyone about this place and you two do all the work. I get a third of the profits for being quiet."

“Henry wasn’t taking any money out of it,” protested Ralph. “He was going to take product for Jessica. Jeremiah, as well. He’s supposed to take it for his glaucoma. I put up all of the money for this.”

“Well now you have more to sell. Of course, that’s assuming I don’t tell the deputies where this is.”

“I could tell them your mother killed Henry.”

“Hah. Like they would believe you? You, who are the other, better and more logical suspect?”

I was inside, now, through the laundry room and into the other end of the trailer. I took a chance looking around the corner.

"Here." I heard the clinking of glass. "Let's drink to our new partnership."

"You drink beer?" Ralph's voice was incredulous.

"Once in a while. You go water plants or whatever it was you were talking about Henry doing. I'll just settle here and wait for you." Justine assured him. "I'll put the gun away now that we have a deal."

Ralph disappeared into what had been a bedroom but was now a greenhouse. Justine settled at a 1950's style wooden kitchen table in the kitchen. I saw her open two beer bottles and then dump several pills into one of them.

Justine whispered to herself "and Jeremiah will have even more to share with me when you are gone, in suicidal remorse, for killing Henry." She gave a triumphant smile.

I gasped and Buddy barked at the same time.

Justine whirled around and shot wildly at the doorway where she had heard me. I shouted out to make her think there were more people with me. "She's got a gun!"

Kind of stupid, I know, had anyone really been there, they would have heard it! I threw my phone across the room to startle her. It was the only thing I had to throw. She shot after it and I took the opportunity to dart across the hallway to the front room, where I knew there had to be another door to the outside. Ralph appeared out of nowhere and I barreled into him. He wrapped a big hand around each of my upper arms and held me up to where my feet barely touched the ground.

I kicked and struggled while he got his surprise under control.

"Patty?"

"She put pills in your beer, you dumbass – don't trust her." I twisted again just as Justine came into the hallway and shot toward me.

Ralph let go abruptly and fell slowly to the floor. Another round hit the wall behind my head and I threw myself past Ralph and into the living room.

The lights flashed on and Deputy Boatright bellowed in his best no-nonsense-I'm-in-charge voice "Stop right there!"

Another shot whizzed right past him. Another shot missed me by inches and I screamed and covered my head with my bullet-proof arms. Deputy Johnson tackled Justine from behind, wrenching the gun from her hand.

Buddy barked and barked and barked. I had to get to him.

"My dog!"

Detective Boatright was on the radio getting an ambulance for Ralph, sending a unit to Jeremiah's house, and requesting another vehicle for back-up. As he spoke, he headed out the door and toward the barking. He untied Buddy and let him run to me.

I was covered with furry golden love, and as I wrapped my arms around him, he danced with concern at my tears.

“I believe there are a couple of others also worried about you.” Detective Danny informed me. "They’re at the gate unless they don’t follow directions any better than you do. Actually, I know they don’t, or they wouldn’t be here at all. Don’t leave the premises, but you’d better go see them.”

A tearful Cheyanne was hanging onto the chain link fence. Rose was wringing her hands next to her. Rose ran forward to hug me and Cheyanne hugged us both. Then Cheyanne hauled back and slugged me. “Don’t EVER do that again! If Rose hadn’t known where this place was, we would never have made it in time!”

I just cried and hugged my dog and then hugged them both again.

"What is going on out here, anyway? I just saw you headed across the road and behind Rose's place. She saw you, and saw me running after. Whatever hunch you had, she had as well! We took her car and she told 911 where to go." Cheyanne was finally calm enough to ask what was going on.

I poked around in my pocket for a tissue and Rose handed me one. I blew my nose and pulled down the tailgate to Rose's SUV. My knees were shaky and I needed to sit. I hauled my dog up with me.

"It's a grow house. Ralph, Jeremiah and Henry were growing marijuana back here. Jeremiah and Henry just wanted the product. Ralph supplied the money and would make a profit on selling the rest." I sighed.

"It really had nothing to do with Henry's death. Jessica killed Henry accidentally. She was angry about the jewelry Henry sold to finance their trip and pay the doctors they saw. I suspect he sold the jewelry to a woman and Jessica just didn't understand."

"I have it recorded on my phone." I reached into my pocket. "Damn. I threw it at Justine."

Just then Justine was forcibly removed from the building. "You bitch! You ruined everything. His suicide would have settled the matter with the insurance company!"

She jerked again and one of the deputies almost lost hold of her. He tightened his grip and the deputies and I were all instructed by Justine to perform various stunts that were anatomically doubtful.

I headed back in after my phone. Deputy Johnson grabbed at me as I scuttled past him.

Ralph was sitting in the same chair Justine had been in. Detective Boatright was wearing gloves and screwing the lid back on the bottle of beer that had been doctored for Ralph.

"WHAT are you doing back in here?"

I meekly pointed to a corner. "My phone. It was on record when I threw it over there."

"Good. It will verify I told you to get out of here and stay at the gate."

He reached for it and slid it into a paper sack.

"Now. Get out of here," he instructed me again.

"Hey Patty," Ralph called out to me. "I was the one who started calling you Potato Woman. I'm sorry."

A preview of Birds, Bees and RVs →

BIRDS, BEES and RVs

"Molly has lived here for twenty years and has played Bingo for most of that time. She comes faithfully and cheers for everyone who wins."

We nodded. Everyone liked Molly. She handed out tiny gifts to people. Mostly things they didn't keep, but it's the thought that counted.

"We were talking about it. She hasn't won in a very long time; years, that we can figure. We suspect it's because she has slowed down some and her hearing isn't the best, so she misses some of the calls.

Obviously, that makes winning almost impossible." Doris shifted her weight as she stalled. "We have decided that she should win the first cover-all game tonight."

Cheyanne and I looked at each other. To say we were surprised would be an understatement; not so much at the plan as at the source of the plan. Martha and her bunch were notoriously mean not only to other people but even to each other.

Neither of us was slow on the uptake, however. "Okay. So no one calls their bingos when they get them. Sooner or later she will have to call one. It might be a good idea to have someone sit next to her and conveniently point out any numbers she misses. It's possible she misses enough that Sally could call all of the numbers and she still wouldn't bingo." Cheyanne pointed out.

Doris gave a huge sigh of relief. "We weren't sure you two would play along."

Well, that was insulting. Especially since it was said so casually. I didn't think Doris meant it that way, but Martha would have.

Doris started to stand, a laborious process for her. "That was a good idea. She always sits in the back. I'll tell her I need to be close to the back and the bathroom tonight, and will sit next to her."

Not only had we been included in the plan - but Doris was going to follow Cheyanne's suggestion.

I looked at Cheyanne after Doris had gone, then I stood and went to the clubhouse door and looked outside.

"What were you looking for?" Cheyanne asked, curiously.

"A blue moon."

Molly had tears running down her face as Doris read her numbers back after her bingo. Most of us had simply not daubed several numbers on purpose, but a few of us were obsessive compulsive enough that we couldn't help it.

Alright, I don't know how many of us were that compulsive or if it was just me. I just had to mark them, just had to. I did not, however, have to call bingo or raise my hand. I also tucked the used sheets into my pockets to dispose of at home.

* * *

I was nuking a diet frozen dinner in the microwave and twisting the top off of a meal-replacement milkshake to drink with it when a siren tore through the park, rending the peace and quiet.

The flashing lights of an ambulance flashed intermittently between homes, trees and community buildings. It stopped on the dark side of the park, in the road right between Marianne and Quinn's home and the clubhouse, diagonally across the street from them.

Albert and I set off at a trot - well, I trotted. Albert winked out - along with a dozen other residents to see what was up.

Marianne was standing at the back of the carport, her cell phone in her hand.

There was no sign of Quinn, he was probably in the middle of things...

Please consider leaving me a review on Amazon or on Goodreads. Reviews are our lifeblood as authors!

Find me at:
https://www.amazon.com/author/maryluscholl

ABOUT THE AUTHOR

Mary Lu Scholl kissed the Blarney Stone and has never looked back.
Retired and living in the paradise of West Central Florida, on the Nature Coast, she writes cozy mysteries for both men and women. She lives with her mom and a cat, around the corner from her daughter.
Family is steadily migrating toward the warm climate and she looks forward to having everyone close.

TRAILER PARK TRAVAILS
PATTY DECKER COZY MYSTERIES

Camper Catastrophe (Book 1)

www.amazon.com/dp/B07MHV48PH

Mobile Mayhem (Book 2)

www.amazon.com/dp/B07MWBL8P

Birds, Bees and RVs (Book 3)

www.amazon.com/dp/B07PM8Z35H

Trailer Trauma (Book 4)

www.amazon.com/dp/B07YCSS9GS

Modular Murder (Book 5)

www.amazon.com/dp/B084T817MG

Corpse in the Clubhouse (Book 6)

www.amazon.com/dp/B08NJ6B2WF

Restless Retirement (Book 7)

www.amazon.com/dp/B093FWNRGY

Soon! Motorhome Motives (Book 8)

www.amazon.com/dp/B09CP1FF29

Eventually, Patty encounters Bernie Murphy.
Bernie lives nearby and that's where Nature Coast Calamities pick up.
With a hint of Irish Folklore,

NATURE COAST CALAMITIES

BERNIE MURPHY COZY MYSTERIES

Lecanto Leprechaun (Book 1)

www.amazon.com/dp/B09ZKNVL49

Big Foot and the Bentley (Book 2)

www.amazon.com/dp/B0B7QHJKM2

InverNessie (Book 3)

www.amazon.com/dp/B0BCHCSX3B

And – coming up soon - a story about manatees, mermaids and murder!

Printed in Great Britain
by Amazon